D0065877

L.E. SMOOT MEMORIAL LIBRARY
KING GEORGE, VA. 22485

THE
Joker
AND THE
Thief

THE
Joker
AND THE
Thief

RAYMOND OBSTFELD

**Delacorte
Press**

L.E. SMOOT MEMORIAL LIBRARY
KING GEORGE, VA. 22485

Published by
Delacorte Press
Bantam Doubleday Dell Publishing Group, Inc.
666 Fifth Avenue
New York, New York 10103

Copyright © 1993 by Raymond Obstfeld

All rights reserved. No part of this book may be reproduced or transmitted in any form or by any means, electronic or mechanical, including photocopying, record-ing, or by any information storage and retrieval system, without the written permission of the Publisher, except where permitted by law.

The trademark Delacorte Press® is registered in the U.S. Patent and Trademark Office.

Library of Congress Cataloging in Publication Data

Obstfeld, Raymond [date of birth]
    The joker and the thief / by Raymond Obstfeld.
        p.   cm.
    Summary: As he becomes involved with a tough, intelligent teenager who has escaped from a juvenile detention center, seventeen-year-old Eric begins to examine his well-planned life and his relationships with his girlfriend and his divorced parents.
    ISBN 0-385-30855-8
    [1.   Self-perception—Fiction.   2.   Interpersonal   relationships—Fiction. 3. Family problems—Fiction. 4. Prisoners—Fiction.] I. Title.
PZ7.O157Jo   1993
[Fic]—dc20   92-9823
                                                                          CIP
                                                                          AC

Interior design by Christine Swirnoff

Manufactured in the United States of America

February 1993

10 9 8 7 6 5 4 3 2 1

BVG

To Justin,
Megan,
and Matt Aakers,
my volleyball, movie, and taco pals.

And to my friend
Peter Dorey,
the king of the Lost Boys.

*"There must be some way out of here," said the joker
to the thief.
"There's too much confusion, I can't get no relief."*

—BOB DYLAN
"ALL ALONG THE WATCHTOWER"

1

Twelve *mud-splattered men* and a dark-haired woman stood in a loose circle around my car. They stared at me through the windshield without budging, without even blinking. Two of the men held shotguns, though not pointing them at anything in particular. One bearded man with no front teeth carried a baseball bat, a fat Louisville Slugger. The wood was pocked with dozens of deep nicks, the kind you get from batting stones, not balls. He just stood there, staring at me, tapping the bat against his leg. Another man, a skinny fellow with a long scythe-shaped scar on his cheek, whispered something to the dark-haired woman and she laughed. When she laughed she threw her head back and her long black hair fell away from her face and I could see she wasn't really a woman. Just a girl, about seventeen. My age.

She whispered something back to the guy with the scar and he nodded. Both of them grinned at me.

"Hey, kid," she said, heading for me. "Wanna ask you something."

My left foot held the clutch pinned to the floorboard. The gear shift was in first. My right foot rested against the gas pedal, just enough to keep the engine humming. I thought about popping the clutch and making a run for it, but no way could I move the car without hitting a couple of them. I was scared enough without getting them mad at me.

The girl leaned her hip against the car, then slowly walked toward me, sliding her hip along the left fender as she got closer. She was wearing button-fly jeans and I could see the stripe of brown dirt collecting on her hip. She didn't seem to mind.

"Ask you something, okay?" she said. She smiled so prettily that I started to smile back, except I caught a flicker of sunlight off one of the shotguns. After that my jaw tightened so hard it would've taken a crowbar to pry even a frown out of me.

"Hey," she repeated. "You're not stupid, are you? Retarded or something?"

I looked over at the old gas station attendant who'd just filled my tank and given me back three bucks and a quarter out of a twenty. He looked away and started counting cans of Quaker State motor oil that were stacked next to the pump. No help there.

I should've paid more attention, but I'd been so busy writing the mileage and gallons in this little red notebook my father had given me. It was the price I had to pay for his lending me the car this weekend. He was a fanatic about getting good mileage. As soon as the car dropped below 25 mpg he traded it in for a new one. He's not cheap or anything, just insists on getting what he calls "full value." It was a pain, but I didn't mind too much. Anyway, that's why I hadn't noticed them coming out of the weeds behind the gas station. That damn notebook.

I heard a tapping on the windshield and I looked up. Her knuckles were pressed against the glass. She had a slight sunburn across the bridge of her nose, but that didn't interfere with her being pretty. Nothing could, even if it tried. She made a cranking motion with her hand and pointed at my window.

I rolled down the window about a sixteenth of an inch. Enough to slip a postcard through as long as it didn't have a stamp on it. "What?" I said.

This cracked her up. She started laughing, looking over her shoulder at Scarface. He was laughing, too, a little. But he was also staring at me.

"Sure you can hear me?" she teased.

"What?" I said. "Can't hear you." I could hear her okay, but I wanted to stall for a couple of seconds, hoping my nervousness would go away. I reached over and turned off the air conditioner. Then I ejected the tape. It was some old Motown stuff of my dad's. He had a whole case of oldies in the car. Stuff like *The Rockin' '60s* and *The British Invasion,* junk like that. I don't usually play them, but the tape I'd made especially for this trip had gotten eaten by the tape deck. Half of it lay twisted and unspooled on the seat next to me, along with a jar of Planters honey-roasted peanuts, a Texaco map of Virginia, and a typed letter from my girlfriend with her neatly drawn map leading me to her parents' cabin. That's where we were supposed to be spending the weekend. Unknown to everybody. All I had to do was find Bishop's Road.

Taking those extra seconds was a good idea. When I faced her again a puddle of sweat was soaking the back of my shirt, but at least my stomach wasn't slam-dancing against my ribs. "What's the question?"

"Seen a kid hiking along the road?"

"A kid?"

"About seventeen. This tall." She held her hand about ten inches above her own head. My height.

"Nope."

"Red hair. Along this road."

"I haven't seen anyone."

She frowned. "You sure?"

I nodded.

She looked back at the others and shook her head. The man with the scar came toward me. My foot tapped involuntarily against the gas pedal and the motor growled a little.

"Relax, son," he said. His voice was quiet and friendly.

"This is Jim Forrest," the girl said. "Reverend Forrest."

"Sheriff Forrest right now," he said. He smiled at me. "Doesn't say much for the separation of church and state around here, eh, son?"

I shrugged. This didn't seem the right time for a social-science debate.

"Thing is, son, we're looking for a boy. About your size and build, I'd guess. Escaped from the juvenile detention a few miles from here. Figured he'd make for the road and try to hitch his way out. He's wearing jeans and a denim shirt."

"I didn't see anybody," I said.

He looked me in the eye and I noticed now that the scar on his cheek didn't look like a scythe so much as the curl of an ocean wave, like on Ocean Spray cranberry juice. "You sure? Jeans and denim shirt. A stenciled number over the left pocket."

"I haven't seen anybody. What's he done?"

He smiled, patted the roof of the car, then faced the

others. "Kid hasn't seen him. Let's check out the woods again."

They all started walking away. No one spoke.

"Hey," I called to the girl. She turned around. "What are you going to do to him when you catch him?"

She shrugged. "If it were up to me, I'd cut his heart out and stuff the hole with manure." She ran to catch up to the reverend or sheriff or whatever he was. She wore hiking boots that laced all the way up her calves.

I watched them wade through the dry, waist-high weeds toward the woods. The guys with shotguns held them high over their heads the way soldiers in movies always do when they're marching through swamps. The toothless guy with the Louisville Slugger kept swinging at the weeds as he walked, as if he were batting homer after homer.

I quickly drove away, cranking up the air-conditioning until I felt a chill on my neck. I popped in Dad's Four Seasons tape even though I like that one least of them all. But Frankie Valli's falsetto is the only thing I can hear over the air conditioner fan.

It didn't take too long to find Bishop's Road. Didra's little hand-drawn map was perfect, as usual. Everything was accurately marked, right down to the peeling billboard for Chesterfield cigarettes. The map said: CHESTERFIELD SIGN. Do they even make that brand anymore? She'd used a ruler to draw the roads and three different colored pens to indicate state, county, and federal roads.

I'd made pretty good time from Washington, D.C., even considering the delay back at the gas station with the Beverly Hillbillies. Didra wasn't due from the airport for another couple of hours, which would give me a chance to chop some wood and build a romantic fire, maybe scatter some pillows around. You know, set the mood.

Everything had to be special this weekend.

Our first weekend since she'd gone off to college.

Our first weekend totally alone.

That's why I was surprised when I drove up to the cabin and saw the front door wide open and a kid outside. A kid about seventeen, in jeans and a denim shirt with a number stenciled across the left pocket, chopping wood on the porch.

He looked up as I braked to a halt. That's when I noticed the blood running down his cheek.

2

H*e slung the big double-edged ax* up over his shoulder and started down the porch steps toward me. I could see now that the blood on his cheek had dried into a dripping shape, like paint around the rim of a paint can. There were other cuts, too, on his forehead, across his arms, along the side of his neck. And his shirt was shredded in half a dozen places.

I guess I should have jammed the gas pedal right then and spun the hell out of there. But there was something in the way he was walking toward me, not rushing like some chain-saw-massacre madman, just strolling casually with a slight grin, like he was coming over to say hi to an old buddy from summer camp. I don't know how to explain it; it was almost as if I'd be rude to leave. I know it sounds nuts, but I've never been very good at making decisions under pressure anyway. Just ask Coach Williams. During practice games, I was the top scorer on our varsity basketball team. Hook shot, lay-up, one-handed pump, I never missed. But come game time, I could barely dribble. The coach tried everything to help me get over my problem: biofeedback machines, visualization exercises, even had some psychology professor pal of his from the university come over and try to hypnotize me. Nothing worked.

"What's that crap you're listenin' to?" the kid with the ax asked.

"The Four Seasons. It's the only thing I can hear over the air conditioner."

"Air conditioner? *Air conditioner?*" He snorted with disgust. "Ain't you heard about the hole in the ozone layer, man? You're gonna give us all skin cancer."

He turned around and walked back up to the porch. With one hand he whipped the ax from his shoulder with such velocity, the sharp head embedded into a log. He sat down on the porch, leaned his head back against a pile of wood he'd just cut, and closed his eyes. As if I weren't even there.

I didn't know how to react. Part of me was relieved. I mean, I'd half expected him to come charging at me with that ax. Part of me was surprised. I didn't expect a guy like this to start spouting off about the ozone layer, to even know there *was* an ozone layer. But part of me, the largest part, was angry. Angry that he'd dismissed me as a threat so easily. We were about the same height and build—I could've tried to make a citizen's arrest. I'd wrestled on junior varsity before sprouting up to my current height of 6'1". And I'd been in a few playground fights in my day and held my own. Sure, that was a long time ago, but he didn't know that. He couldn't know what I would do. I might have even driven off and told the authorities. Neither possibility seemed even to occur to him.

I got out of the car and walked a few steps toward the

porch. Believe me, I had no idea what I was doing, why I didn't just drive off and let that hick posse deal with this escaped criminal. But, for one thing, I didn't want Didra showing up here while I was gone.

"They told you about me, huh?" he said, without opening his eyes.

"Pardon?" I said.

"Told you 'bout me escaping. From the detention camp."

"I saw some people looking for you. They asked me some questions."

He opened his eyes, squinted at me, then started to laugh. "Yeah, I'll bet they did. I'll just bet they did."

"Look," I said, trying to sound decisive, "you can't stay here. I'm meeting someone here. They should be driving up any time now."

" 'They'?" He smiled, closed his eyes again, leaned his head back. "So that's why you didn't drive right off to fetch the reverend sheriff. Afraid 'they' might arrive."

I didn't answer him. There was a cockiness in his tone I didn't like, as if he knew something about me, some secret.

"Suppose," he said. "Suppose your friend already got here, say half an hour ago. Suppose I already had my way with her, you know, the way desperadoes like me do. And then suppose, not wanting her to talk, I'd taken Mr. Ax here to her and chopped her up like a spinach salad? Then what?"

My heart made a fist so tight I nearly doubled over from the pain. I had to suck each breath into my lungs with great effort, as if I were breathing through eight layers of wet wool. Reason it out, I heard my father's crisp voice in my head. Dad teaches logic and philosophy at the university. To him there's no problem that can't be solved by mathematical logic.

"You didn't murder anyone, at least not with that ax," I said.

The red-haired boy opened his eyes and looked at me, as if noticing me for the first time. "Oh, yeah? What makes you so smart?"

"You're wearing the clothes you escaped in. If you'd axed anyone, there would be blood on your clothes, lots of blood. The little that's on them now is undoubtedly from your own wounds."

"Okay, Sherlock, maybe I didn't ax her. Maybe I just tied her up and had some fun." He licked his lips in an exaggerated leer and laughed.

I shook my head. "She would have arrived by cab. There are no other fresh tire marks here. Only from my car." I gestured at the dirt driveway in front of the cabin.

He looked at the dirt, straining to see what I was pointing at. Actually, I had no idea if there were any other tire tracks or if another car would even leave any. But I held his gaze with a stern glare of my own.

He nodded. "I think you're jerkin' me around, sport."

"Frankly, what you think doesn't really matter much."

He leaned his elbows on the porch railing and looked off at the horizon. Tree-cluttered mountains surrounded the cabin. Big green trees everywhere. The cabin was the only building for miles. Didra's father owned a couple of hundred acres in each direction to insure his privacy. Privacy was very important to Mr. Lester.

"Aren't you gonna ask, sport?" the red-haired kid said.

"Ask what?"

"What I did. My horrible crime. How I got myself locked up like that."

I wasn't really thinking about that right then. I was staring at the numbers stenciled across his breast pocket, thinking it an odd coincidence that they were very close to my locker combination at school. If you reversed the last two digits, it would be the same. I don't believe in coincidences or signs or anything like that—they're not logical—but for some reason, those numbers shook me a little. I couldn't stop thinking about them.

Mistaking my silence for fear, I guess, he said, "Don't sweat it, man. I didn't kill nobody. Just a little destruction of private property."

I walked closer to him, maybe to prove I wasn't afraid. "You'd better go. When my friend arrives, she . . . Well, you might frighten her."

"And I don't frighten you?"

"I don't want any trouble. Whatever is going on between you and those people is none of my business. I'm just here for the weekend."

"To get a little pussy."

I flushed. "You'd better go."

He nodded. "Yeah. I guess I should thank you for not turning me in or anything." He was standing at the top of the porch steps, I was at the bottom. He reached his hand down to shake.

"That's all right," I said, taking his hand.

The instant his hand grasped mine, he tightened his grip like a shark's jaws slamming onto a tuna. He yanked, pulling me off-balance into the porch steps. I fell face down, banging my knee on the edge of one of the steps. The red-haired kid leaped over my prone body and raced for my father's car.

The keys were still in the ignition.

I scrambled, trying to get to my feet. My knee ached as if someone had hammered a nail into it. I took a step and my leg splayed out from under me, dropping me to one knee. I dragged myself upright again just as he tried to start the engine. The car gets good mileage, but it needs to be babied a little when you first start it. In his hurry, he flooded it. I hobbled a few steps toward the car, but I could see I'd never make it in time. He turned the key again. The engine sputtered, then caught. He gunned the gas and smoke fired out of the muffler.

Within seconds he'd be gone.

I dashed up onto the porch, hopping on one leg, grabbed the ax, and jerked it free from the log. I jumped down off the porch, bypassing the four steps. The impact sent a jolt of pain up my knee that seemed to disintegrate the whole leg. I collapsed to the ground. He spun the car toward me, circling in the narrow driveway. The fat black tires spit dirt and gravel into my face, just missing crunching me by inches.

Still flat on my back in the dirt, I swung the ax into the front tire as the car sped by me. The tire exploded, sending the car into a shaky tailspin. The front fender scraped a couple of the large boulders that lined the driveway. The fender hooked onto a boulder, dragging it a few feet before the front of the car smashed into a thick pine tree. The horn blared steadily.

I struggled to my feet. The red-haired kid's head rested against the horn. This time the blood on his face was fresh.

I limped toward the car and tried to figure how I would write this in my father's little red mileage book.

3

In *my whole life,* I have only ever seen my father lose his temper once.

Dad's calm demeanor in the face of crisis is legendary in our neighborhood, at the university where he teaches, and among family and friends. He refuses to get upset about things over which he has no control. Some people appreciate that characteristic more than others. Aunt Judith, my mother's sister, used to call Dad "Robby the Robot" from some old sci-fi movie from the fifties she and Mom watched as kids. She'd say things like, "What's Robby the Robot been up to lately?" Then she'd crack up.

A few years ago, when I was in ninth grade and about half my current size, I came home from an algebra test with an F. Teaching logic and philosophy involves a lot of mathematics, so Dad is no slouch in that department. In fact, a few times my math teachers have asked for his help solving some complicated math problems. Anyway, I knew he'd find out sooner or later about the F, especially since I was a straight A student, so I told him right away.

He sat in his den and studied my exam without any expression. Gerry and the Pacemakers were on the stereo singing something like "Don't Let the Sun Catch You Crying." For a smart guy, Dad sure has dumb taste in music. When he was finished looking over the test, he handed it back to me and said, "These answers are correct."

"I know," I said. "I got the F for cheating."

He nodded, again without any sign of surprise, although this was the first time I'd ever been accused of cheating. "Did you cheat?" he asked.

"I didn't copy off anybody," I said, hedging.

He waited.

"But I let Stan Cooley copy off me."

"Oh?" The record ended, so he reached over and shut off the stereo. "Why?"

I hated that question, especially from him. He wasn't the kind of parent who would accept "I dunno" or "Because." He wanted reasons, clearly articulated and supported with specific examples. It was like a math test all over again. If I'd shown it to Mom, she'd have cried and asked me why I was doing this to her.

"Why did you allow Stan Cooley to copy?"

"Because he said he'd beat the shit out of me if I didn't let him."

Again he nodded. Foul language in the interest of authenticity was permissible. "Did you believe he would?"

"Yes."

"Why?"

"He's beaten up kids before. Last month he chipped Phil Steuben's tooth." I pointed to one of my front teeth as a visual aid. For what I'd saved him in dentist's bills alone he should be grateful.

"And you determined he had the ability to beat you up?"

I nodded vigorously. "He's two years older, fifty pounds heavier. He's a tackle on the football team."

"I see." My father removed his reading glasses and rubbed his eyes. He had a book open in his lap. Something by Spinoza, one of his favorite philosophers. "Were there any other alternatives? Telling the teacher, for example."

"Get real, Dad."

He gave me a sharp look.

I rephrased my answer. "The alternative was unacceptable. It would have resulted in disdain from my peers."

"So you thought it would be better to risk failing your exam rather than risk getting beat up or enduring disdain from your peers?"

"Yes, sir."

He put his glasses back on. "Okay then. Thank you for telling me, Eric. Go wash up for dinner. I've made something special." This was before the divorce, but even then he did most of the cooking, because his teaching schedule allowed him to come home earlier than Mom.

I should have felt relief and bolted out of there. But I knew something was wrong. "Dad?"

"Yes?"

"What would you have done?"

He looked up from his book. This time he closed the book. One of the weird things about my dad is that he never uses a bookmark. He's always reading, three or four books at a time, but he never needs bookmarks. He always knows right where he's left off. Anyway, he closed his Spinoza book and stood up. "It doesn't matter what I would have done. You assessed the situation, you reasoned your options, you made a decision. You acted based on your analysis of the data. I can't fault you there, son."

I smiled. "Then I made the logical choice?"

"I didn't say that."

I sighed with frustration. "Can't you just tell me for once? Just flat out say yes or no?"

"No, I can't," he said. "And you know why."

I recited as if it were the Boy Scout oath: "Because opinions aren't important, only the process by which we arrive at those opinions."

"That's right."

I thought for a moment. "So what you're saying is that by letting Stan copy off me, I'm saying that he can copy off me any time he wants. Which means I'll always be risking flunking. Right?"

"And?"

"And . . ." I thought a moment. "And I'm risking losing something more valuable than a beating. So my action wasn't logical at all."

He smiled at me again and squeezed my shoulder affectionately. "Let's eat."

Now, most of my friends don't understand about my dad. They think the fact that he doesn't yell at me about things is weird. Some of them call him Mr. Spock; you know, from *Star Trek*. When I was younger, I used to wonder if his lack of hollering meant a lack of caring. Especially since my mom yelled enough for the both of them. He never scolded me for making stupid choices like my friends' parents did. As long as I could explain my reasons, he supported my decisions, even when it was obvious he didn't agree with them. When you stop and think about it, that's a lot harder on a parent than just telling a kid what to do.

Which brings us to the time my dad lost his temper.

Dad had once been a promising tennis amateur. He has cardboard boxes stuffed full of trophies from high school and college. He tried to throw them all out once, but Mom wouldn't let him. She wanted to keep them on display in the den. They compromised by storing them in the attic. Dad and Mom used to play doubles back then, every weekend at the university with other faculty couples.

It was after one of those doubles matches that things got weird. They were playing Dr. Tom Askers, who was Mom's department chairperson. They both taught art at the university. Dr. Askers's partner was a young female student, nineteen, I think. Dr. Askers always had some young coed partner, which Mom and Dad used to talk about when they got home. Mom always wondered what a man Dr. Askers's age was doing with girls twenty years younger.

"You're the same age as Tom," Dad always pointed out logically.

After that there was usually a long silence and a lot of slamming cupboards.

I used to wonder how Dr. Askers hooked such beautiful girls. He was overweight, sloppy, with long, unkempt hair, mostly gray. Still, every weekend he had yet another gorgeous date.

Here's what happened: The four of them came home after tennis. I was in my bedroom watching a tape the coach had made of our last wrestling meet. I heard them out there in the kitchen, Mom passing cold cans of soft drink around. Dr. Askers's voice was booming, as usual. I decided to go out, scope the girl, see what the argument would be about later.

I was halfway to the kitchen when I heard Mom laugh and say, "Men. They're always trying to recapture their youth."

Dr. Askers's bimbo *du jour* giggled in agreement.

And Dad yelled, I mean *yelled*, "That is the stupidest damn statement. Men aren't trying to *recapture* anything. They're trying not to lose what they've had all along: the pure delight in discovery, the fascination with everything around them. It's inside every boy—and man. The sheer pleasure of skipping a stone across a pond can never be duplicated by buying a damn BMW."

"Whoa, Jim, speak for yourself," Dr. Askers said, chuckling. "I love my Beemer."

"Jim," Mom said, her voice a little ragged. "What's gotten into you?"

The weird thing is that I always thought that when Dad would lose his temper, it would be about something important, like me crashing the car or something. Not over some dopey conversation about recapturing youth and skipping stones. Even when they got the divorce, I never saw him lose his temper.

Even when Mom married Dr. Askers and they moved to Hawaii.

4

The *hard part was* stopping the bleeding.

The ice maker in the refrigerator had been shut off, since this wasn't the season the Lesters used the cabin. Naturally, it was a frost-free model, so I couldn't chip any ice off the sides. However, there were a couple of boxes of frozen peas, which I grabbed.

When I limped back to the living room, the red-haired kid was still stretched out on the sofa, where I'd dumped him after carrying him in over my shoulder. He was still unconscious. I propped his head up with two huge pillows that had been stacked on the floor next to the fireplace. The gash on his forehead had soaked through the toilet paper I'd stuck there and was now dripping along his nose, leaving a thin bloody stripe on his cheek. I peeled the soggy red clump from his skin. The cut looked serious, about as long and wide as a caterpillar. I dabbed the wound with some perox-ide I'd found in the bathroom, and pressed a box of Birds

Eye frozen peas against it. Instantly his eyes snapped open and he grabbed my wrist.

"What the hell are you doing?" His voice was alert and his grip was surprisingly strong, as if he were used to bolting awake at the slightest disturbance.

"RICE," I told him.

"What?"

"Rest, Ice, Compression, Elevation. RICE. It'll stop the bleeding and bring down the swelling."

He snorted, releasing his stranglehold on my wrist. "I shoulda known. A Girl Scout."

"Hold it tight against the skin," I said, demonstrating again.

When he didn't make any move to take the box, I let it go and it slid down his cheek, leaving a skid mark of watery pink blood. He picked up the box and placed it against his wound. He closed his eyes.

"The car's out of commission," I said, "so I'll have to call an ambulance. You need some stitches."

He didn't say anything, so I went over to the phone next to the bookshelf. "Does 911 work out here?" I asked.

Again he didn't answer. I dialed 911. And I mean dialed. This was an old-fashioned wall phone, the kind you'd see in gangster films where they'd put a black cup to their ear and talk into a funnel. Mr. Lester's idea of rustic charm.

I put the cup to my ear. There was no sound, no dial tone. I dialed again. Still nothing.

"I cut the lines outside," he said casually, eyes still closed.

"Why didn't you tell me before I dialed?"

He grinned. "I'm delirious. Can't you tell?"

I limped across the room and flopped down into the big easy chair next to the sofa. I pressed the other box of peas against my aching knee. The chair smelled of Mr. Lester, his expensive cologne, his imported cigars. Just sitting there made me feel powerful. Decisive. "We'll wait for Didra," I told him. "The cab driver can take you to the proper authorities."

"The proper authorities," he mimicked, making a spinsterish face. "You say that like someone who's always been on the right side of them. Ain't that right, Girl Scout?"

My face flushed. Not with anger this time, but with embarrassment. I have always been a model student, son, grandson, stepson, employee, boyfriend. Except for the occasional lapse—the *F* on that algebra test, the time I soaped Mr. Bingham's windows during Halloween—I've pretty much been the one who teachers always mention when chastising some disruptive student whispering in class, or store supervisors refer to when scolding a lazy cashier for not asking which sauce the customers want with their Chicken McNuggets. They point and say those deadly words, "Why can't you be more like Eric." Naturally, that kind of thing keeps the number of my friends down to a manageable size. But even those few friends have parents who eventually get around to proclaiming the same horrid line. Then, like a magic curse, those friends disappear too. I don't blame them. And it's not that I've made a conscious effort to please adults or anything. It's just the way I am. The rules of life are very clear, and if you follow them you get along with a minimum of fuss. Which cuts down on a lot of high-pressure decision-making. Of course, there is such a thing as going overboard, I guess. Even my father has encouraged me to relax more, act my age. As he put it, "to spend more time skipping stones across ponds."

Well, sure, I guess I would if I could. I just don't know how to be any different from how I am. I have a theory that no matter how you act or what you do, people are always going to tell you to act differently or do something else. More this way or less that way. It's as if they didn't really care what you did, only that you recognize that you could be wrong, that we all are imperfect. Hell, I didn't need anybody telling me that; I already knew. Anyway, maybe Dad was right, I did need to loosen up.

That's why I'd arranged this romantic weekend with Didra. We'd been dating for over a year, since back when I was still a junior and she was a senior. We met during the senior class play, Shakespeare's *A Midsummer Night's Dream*. I played Oberon and she played Titania, my wife. We were the king and queen of the faeries, for which I took a lot of ribbing, even though we played real faeries with magic powers and stuff. Like wizards in Dungeons & Dragons. At first we helped each other memorize our lines, then we were snatching kisses behind the scenery during rehearsals. Maybe I'm a slow starter, but we never really got much past the kissing and petting stage. Just a button here, a hand there. Then she went off to college. So I guess you could say that this was supposed to be the weekend I was going to skip stones across the pond.

And now look what happened. A banged-up knee, my dad's tire axed, his car totaled, and an escaped convict on the sofa with a box of frozen peas pressed against his head.

Maybe some people aren't meant to skip stones.

5

"What *exactly did you mean* about the ozone layer?" I said suddenly. Which was weird, because I hadn't even been thinking about that. I mean, why would I?

"What?" He opened his eyes and gave me a cockeyed look.

"When I first drove up. You said something about the ozone layer and the air conditioner. What did you mean?"

He grinned in that annoying way, the one that suggested he knew my secrets. Maybe what annoyed me so much was that I didn't have any secrets. I wish I did.

"You are odd, kid," he said.

"Answer my question," I said.

"Don't you want to get to know each other a little first?"

"No."

"Don't you at least want to swap names?"

"Not really."

"Oh, I get it." He sat up, adjusted the pillows behind

him. "You're afraid of a reverse Stockholm Syndrome. That it?"

"Stop that!"

"What?" He grinned. "Stop what?"

The Stockholm Syndrome. We'd studied that in the psychology class I had at the university last summer. They have a special program that allows students with a certain GPA to take introductory general education courses. That way, by the time we actually enroll full-time, we'll already have stockpiled some credits. By the time I start classes next fall, I'll actually be a sophomore. Then when I transfer to Didra's school, we'll be in the same graduating class. I've planned it all out very logically.

Anyway, the Stockholm Syndrome refers to a terrorist skyjacking a few years ago in which the hostages got so dependent on their kidnappers that they formed an emotional attachment to them, almost like a family. When you think about it, most kids my age feel like they're being held hostage anyway, with no one to pay the ransom. What got me, though, was where this kid from a hillbilly detention camp heard about this stuff.

"Tell me about the ozone layer," I repeated. I wanted to see if he really knew what he was talking about or if he was just a con artist.

"I'm hungry," he said. He tossed the box of frozen peas to me. "Can you cook these up while we're waiting?"

When I reached up to catch the box, I dropped my own box and I missed the one he threw to me too. Both boxes dropped to the floor. I bent over and picked one of them up and pressed it back against my knee.

"Hey, I guess that makes us blood brothers, huh?"

"What are you talking about?"

He pointed at my knee and smiled.

I looked. There was a small tear in the knee of my pants that I hadn't noticed before. There was also a little blood.

"You picked up my box of peas," he said. "It had my blood on it. So when you pressed it against your knee, our blood mixed. That makes us blood brothers. Right, bro?"

I examined the box of peas in my hand. Then I snatched up the other box. "They both have blood on them. You can't tell which is which."

"I can tell, bro."

"Stop calling me that."

"Sibling rivalry already?" He chuckled.

God, he was irritating. I took a deep breath. Logical. Be logical. "Even if I picked up the wrong box, even if our blood did technically mix, that doesn't make us blood brothers. Becoming blood brothers is symbolic. Merely an oral agreement by both parties."

"Like a marriage?"

"Like a contract. And for this contract to be binding, there needs to be a ceremony, a ritual, if you will, in which both parties agree to the conditions, either stated or implied, of such a relationship. We have no such agreement, ergo no relationship."

He shook his head, a crooked smile on his lips. "Man, they must invite you to a lot of parties, just so's you'll talk like that. Give 'em something to laugh at."

My knee still ached, but even though I'd proven logically that we were in no way blood brothers, I didn't much feel like putting the wrong box of peas on my knee. Still, I felt kind of stupid just sitting there with a box of frozen peas in each hand, with him grinning at me as if the fact that I refused to hold one of them against my knee proved his point, no matter how logical I was. So I stood up and started for the kitchen. "Might as well cook them up. I'm getting hungry myself."

I hate peas, so I was really hoping Didra would show up with the cab before I finished cooking them and was forced to eat any. Somehow I knew that if I refused to eat them, he'd have proven something else. I didn't know what, but I didn't want to give him any satisfaction.

The peas were in plastic pouches that you could either boil or microwave. The microwave oven was attached under the cupboard. But since boiling took longer, I got out the pot and filled it with water. I stayed in the kitchen and watched the tiny bubbles form around the edge of the pot. Every once in a while I'd lean over and glance into the living room to make sure the red-haired kid wasn't trying to sneak off, even though I was sure I'd hear him if he tried.

I must've been concentrating too hard on the bubbles, because next thing I knew he was standing in the kitchen doorway asking, "What time do you expect your girlfriend?"

He startled me, not having made any noise, and my hand jerked out and brushed against the hot pot. "Owww!" I waved the back of my hand, which burned as if it had been stung by a dozen hornets.

"Ice would help," he said.

"You think if we had any ice we'd have been using frozen peas!" I hollered.

He smiled. "I guess I'm not as logical as you."

I walked over to the sink and ran the cold water. I didn't wait for it to get cold, I just stuck my hand under the stream. It helped a little. Even through the waterfall I could see a small blister the size of a dime puffed up below the knuckle of my middle finger.

"Hey," he said cheerfully. "You could draw a little face on that blister, then when you gave people the finger, they'd really be confused."

"No, thank you," I said. "I don't want to end up like you."

It was a childish thing to say, something I might have said when I was twelve, perhaps embellished with a few nyah, nyah, nyahs. But it seemed to sober him up some. He dropped his smile and walked back into the living room. I followed, to make sure he wouldn't pull another tiptoe act and escape. I mean, someone had to be responsible for my dad's car. He didn't seem much interested in escaping though. He sat back on the sofa and laid down.

"What do you think they're gonna do when you turn me in?" he said. He sounded as if he already knew the answer.

"Take you to the hospital, I guess. Fix you up."

"There's no hospital for forty miles."

"A doctor then. You've got a doctor around here, don't you?"

He snorted. "Yeah, we got a doctor. At the detention camp."

"Well, then, that's where they'll take you. You need stitches."

"Stitches? What do I need stitches for?"

For a guy who knew about the ozone layer and the Stockholm Syndrome, he sure was acting dumb. "To stop the bleeding, for one thing," I said. "And to prevent scarring."

He laughed loudly. "Scarring? You think I give a rat's ass about scarring?" He reached down and pulled his denim shirt up to his chest. His torso was surprisingly muscular for a kid his age. Knots and ridges of hard muscles protruded. His skin, however, looked like the topographical map of Europe that I'd made for the sixth grade science fair. The one with plaster of paris mountains and lakes. He had scars as lumpy as my Alps. Three or four thin ones wrapped around his ribs and disappeared under his back. A few small ones clustered together in the middle of his chest like a constellation.

And then there was the last one.

It was as large as a walnut, the skin puffed and shiny in a pattern that reminded me of a sunburst. It looked like one of those wax seals royalty used to put on official documents.

These were not normal childhood scars. I have a big wormy one on my back from falling on some broken glass when I was a kid. And I have one at the corner of my eye where Linda Brexel threw a stone at me in third grade. I think I called her a beanpole or something. And there are a few more scars here and there, the origins of which I no longer recall.

But these were nasty-looking, unnatural somehow. The kind that you never forget how you got.

I couldn't take my eyes off the sunburst.

"What happened?" I finally asked. He knew which scar I meant.

"You mean Walter here?" He pulled his shirt down and smiled at me. "Nothing too complicated. Somebody shot me."

I didn't say anything for a minute. I mean, what do you say to a guy who names his scars. Especially ones he got from bullets. His life was so radically different from mine, I felt as if I'd discovered some new species of animal, like I was an explorer and should study this creature for the sake of science.

I don't know how long I was silent. The quiet was interrupted by the sound of a car driving up outside. Tires crunched dirt and gravel. A heavy door opened, then slammed shut. Then Didra's frantic voice called, "Eric, are you okay? What happened to your car? Eric? Eric?"

L.E. SMOOT MEMORIAL LIBRARY
KING GEORGE, VA. 22485

6

Any other time, the concern I heard in Didra's voice would have made me smile. Didra wasn't just my girlfriend, she was also my best friend—the only person I really confided in. I felt like we were two spies surviving on our wits in a cold, foreign country. Sometimes we would go over to the Lincoln Memorial with a camera, pretend to be visiting tourists, and have other tourists snap our photo together.

"Eric?" she called again, her voice getting louder as she neared the front door. "Can you hear me? Are you in there?"

I was about to answer when I felt a panic grenade explode in my stomach, the kind that bombarded me during basketball games. Suddenly I realized I had a decision to make. A few minutes earlier I hadn't even known this situation involved any choices. It had been so clear-cut. Now I was back out on the gym floor with the ball in my hands, the crowd screaming, and two seconds left to win the game. I had to do something.

I looked at him. He laced his fingers behind his head and closed his eyes. I saw the tip of a tattoo stick out from under his sleeve. It looked like it had reptile scales.

I heard a thud on the porch. "Well, he can't be too hurt if he chopped all this wood," Didra said.

"You want me to wait, ma'am?" a man said.

"Maybe you'd better. Until I check things out."

Her shoes clicked against the wooden porch steps.

Well, the cab was here. Our link with civilization. The driver could take the kid back with him, or at the very least use his radio to call the sheriff. Didra and I would be alone, the whole weekend ahead of us. As if nothing had happened.

I looked over at the kid again. A drop of blood was forming at the edge of his wound. It seemed to grow bigger as I stared, like a flower blooming. I thought of the frozen boxes of Birds Eye peas with our blood smeared on them. I looked at my hands; there was dried blood around my fingernails.

Suddenly my mind was made up, though I didn't remember having any say in the decision. I hadn't wrestled with options, plotted consequences, compared alternative scenarios. Logic had abandoned me completely.

I quickly limped across the room and pulled open the front door. Didra stood there with her small suitcase and a paper bag full of groceries. "Hi," I said, smiling, blocking the door.

"My God, Eric. What happened to your car?" She looked down at my knee. "Are you okay?"

"I'm fine. I had a blowout and the car spun out of control. Banged up my knee, that's all."

"Are you sure you're okay?" She placed her hand on my forehead. "No fever."

"It's my knee that got wrecked, not my head." I smiled. "But you can keep your hand there anyway."

"You're crazy," she said. She kissed me on the cheek and looked back at Dad's smashed-up car. "Daddy's going to be pissed about those boulders."

"Yes, I know." I took the bag of groceries from her, but made no move to go inside.

The cab driver was an older man with a grizzled face and suspicious eyes. He looked over at the car, then at me. His eyes were small wet holes pressed between a couple dozen layers of wrinkles, probably from a lifetime of squinting suspiciously at people. "Need anything else, ma'am?"

Didra handed him a twenty-dollar bill. "No, thank you."

He took the twenty without taking his eyes off me. Then he backed away toward his cab. "You need a ride back to the airport, you ask for me. Name's Earl."

"Thank you, Earl," Didra said. Her tone carried with it the unspoken words, *I won't be needing you, please leave.* Didra had that way about her. A way of saying things so that they spoke more than the words. Everybody understood her tones and if asked to repeat the conversation, would probably add the words implied as if she'd really said them. I admired that about her.

Earl drove off and I had a sharp kick of regret in my gut as I saw his cab disappear down the tree-lined road. What the hell had I just done?

"I stopped and bought these on the way," she said, indicating the groceries. "Some steak and wine to make the evening special."

I took her in my free arm and kissed her, hugging her and the grocery bag at the same time. I haven't really kissed that many girls, so I have no way of telling how good a kisser Didra was. All I know is that when we kissed like this, I felt like I was the best person I could be. Like I could go out on the court during the championship finals with three seconds to play. All they had to do was get the basketball to me so I could shoot. No way could I miss. I figured that feeling must be love.

Didra squirmed in my arms, made a sound that vibrated across my lips and echoed in my mouth. I opened my eyes and saw she was staring, wide-eyed, at something behind me. I released her and spun around.

The red-haired kid stood in the doorway. Blood dripped from his open wound, but he was grinning, almost leering. "Hey, bro," he said. "Ain't ya gonna introduce me to your babe?"

7

Why *did I let* the cab leave?

Afterward, I reasoned it out like this: Since I didn't have anything to do with these backwoods hicks or their detention camps or their juvenile delinquents, I didn't have any responsibility to get involved. I was here for a weekend of getting reacquainted with my girlfriend, whom I hadn't seen since she went off to college. Nothing else was any of my business. The red-haired kid would have to leave, of course, but what he did after that was up to him. He could take his chances with his wound and hitchhike out to California. Or he could turn himself in and receive medical attention. It was his choice. Not mine.

For a moment I toyed with the idea of giving him Mom and Dr. Askers's address in Hawaii. He could visit them for a while. Mom would lecture him about how he was breaking his parents' hearts, how he was only hurting himself, how he could turn his life around with proper diet and daily meditation. Dr. Askers would probably toss him a bottle of beer and swap dirty jokes with him.

That's what he tried to do with me when I visited them last Easter break.

I don't know why I went. Mom had been asking me to visit them in Hawaii for over a year, ever since she moved there with Tom. There was no custody problem between my folks. The public schools on Kauai weren't as competitive as the one I was attending. Plus I had already decided to attend the university after graduation. So we all agreed it was best for me to stay in D.C. with Dad. Twice Mom had sent round-trip tickets for me to visit them, but both times I sent them back with some lame excuse about a test or something. Finally, Mom flew back to visit me. She stayed at the house as if nothing had changed among us. Except, she slept in my room and I slept on the couch. Before she left, she made me promise to visit her at Easter.

Dad didn't seem to mind about the trip. He didn't hate Mom, he didn't even hate Dr. Askers, who had been his best friend. In fact, he still talked to Dr. Askers on the phone as much as he did Mom, the two of them gossiping about other faculty members. As if they were still best buddies. The night before I was to leave for Hawaii, I asked him about that.

"Dad, I know you guys are all mature adults and all, but aren't you a little angry about what Mom did to you?"

We were doing the dishes. He didn't like the way the dishwasher cleaned the dishes, so we always did them by hand. Today he was washing and I was drying.

"She didn't do anything to me, Eric."

"Stop me if I'm wrong here, but the way I see it, Mom left you for your best friend."

He scrubbed a stubborn lasagna stain from the metal

pan. "She didn't do that *to* me. She fell in love with someone else. Tom Askers is a good man. They have a lot in common —their art, for example. I don't blame her."

"But Dr. Askers was your best friend." I don't know why, but his lack of anger was getting me angry. I guess I was purposely goading him. "He stole your wife!"

"You can't steal something that doesn't belong to anyone. Your mother didn't 'belong' to me. We loved each other, we still do. It's just that the nature of that love changed."

"Did it change for you? The way you felt about Mom, I mean."

He pushed the lasagna pan back into the sudsy water even though it was clean. He continued to scrub it with the copper cleaner. When he spoke, his voice was so quiet I almost couldn't hear him. "No."

"Then you should be angry at Mom for leaving, for not trying to make it work between you."

He rinsed the pan under the spigot. Water splashed up into his glasses. "Nothing lasts forever, Eric. Not monuments, not governments, not planets, not solar systems. Certainly not human relationships."

"That's depressing."

He turned to me and smiled. "Not really. It's kind of encouraging. Even though people know that nothing lasts, they keep trying. That's a tribute to the indomitable human spirit. I call that uplifting."

"I call that foolish. Logically speaking."

He laughed, flicked three fingers' worth of lemon-scented soapsuds in my face. "You got me there, son."

I scooped some suds in my hand and tossed them in his face. They clung to his glasses like fake snow. *"Now* I got you."

We both laughed and pretty soon I was feeling better about going.

If I'd have known what was going to happen to me in Hawaii, I wouldn't have been laughing so hard.

8

We *were standing* in the kitchen, unpacking groceries and whispering.

"Do something, Eric," Didra said. She stood so close I could feel her breath against my cheek.

"Do what?"

"I don't know. Arrest him."

"How?"

"A citizen's arrest. Under certain circumstances, you're allowed to make a citizen's arrest."

"What if he doesn't want to be arrested?"

She waved her hands with frustration. "I don't know. Tie him up, I guess. I'm sure there's some rope around here someplace. Daddy's very careful about such things, batteries and rope and snake-bite kits." She opened a drawer as if she expected to find rope in it. All she found was some packs of cigarettes her parents must have left. She closed the drawer.

The red-haired kid was in the other room building a fire.

I could hear him in there humming a song that sounded vaguely familiar, tossing some cut wood on the flames. I had the creepy feeling that despite our whispering and his humming, he could hear every word we said.

Didra had listened to my recounting of today's events without interruption. She just continued unpacking the groceries while I talked, occasionally handing me a can of soup or a box of cereal to store away in the cupboard. But I could tell she was absorbing every word. Didra's a journalism major at college, so I was very careful to include as many details as possible. She loves facts. She seems to remember them all, too, because she's better at Trivial Pursuit than anybody I know, including Dad. She's very ambitious too. She was editor of our school newspaper last year and did a terrific job. It was her idea, for example, to add all those computer graphics on the sports page.

After I was done with the who, what, where, when, and how of my story, she put her hand on my arm and asked the real stumper. "Why, Eric?"

"Pardon?"

"Why didn't you have the cab driver call the sheriff on his radio?"

I didn't know how to explain it to her, I suppose because I didn't have a satisfactory explanation for myself. Certainly I couldn't tell her about the blood on the boxes of frozen peas, the bullet scar named Walter, the tip of the tattoo under his cuff, the stenciled number on his shirt that was similar to my locker combination. I knew these were all factors in my decision; I just didn't know how.

All I knew for sure was that the thought of turning him in made me feel queasy. Bad reason, I know, but teachers are always telling you that when you take a test and you're unsure of the answer, go with your first instinct—that's usually the right one. Don't overanalyze. Well, for once, that's what I did.

I reached over and shut off the gas under the boiling water. At least I wouldn't have to eat peas now.

"I don't understand why you didn't do that, Eric," she said.

"It's hard to explain."

"Tell me. I'll try to understand."

I picked at the dried blood on my fingernails. According to my original plan, by now Didra and I should be relaxing in front of that fire, kissing intensely to make up for the past three months apart. "It just didn't seem right, that's all."

Didra sighed. She lifted a box of microwavable popcorn out of the grocery bag. "I flew up from Florida, unknown to my parents, though as soon as they see the airfare charge on their American Express they'll know. Then I drove in a rattle-trap cab that smelled like rotting pig flesh for half an hour, just to spend a romantic weekend with you. And when I get here you tell me we have a guest. The escaped convict who came to dinner."

She can be very witty when she's sarcastic.

"It's not like he's staying," I said. "I just didn't want to turn him in. We'd end up spending our whole weekend at the police station while the sheriff calls our folks."

She stopped unpacking a moment, holding the bottle of white wine in her hand. "Good point. I should have known there'd be a logical explanation for your actions." She smiled. "You're forgiven."

She set the wine down, turned, and rubbed up against me, her hips bumping my hips, her arms circling my waist. She kissed my throat, taking a little of the skin between her teeth playfully. That gave me a little chill behind my ears.

One hand slid down my back, down over my belt, down, down . . .

"You look very different from your photograph," the red-haired kid said from the doorway.

Didra jumped and chomped down on my throat.

"Oww!" I pulled away, touched my fingers to my throat. A little drop of blood. So far today I'd seen more blood than I'd seen my whole life.

"Sorry, sweetheart," she said. "He scared me."

"I did?" The red-haired kid shrugged. "I'm sorry, I didn't mean to. It's just that you two were in here for so long, I thought maybe you sneaked out on me. Made a getaway." He chuckled. "Anyway, Eric failed to introduce us. My name's Griffin Coyle." He held out his hand.

Didra is nothing if not polite. Reluctantly, she shook his hand. "Didra Lester."

"Nice meeting you, Didra." He turned to me and held out his hand. "Griffin Coyle."

I didn't take his hand. Doing so somehow seemed too personal, too intimate. I didn't want this fellow to think we were in any way friends because of what had happened. I turned away and unpacked a couple of liter bottles of Diet 7-Up.

"Come on, Eric," he said. "See? I already know your first name." He turned to Didra and shook his head. "Is he always this stubborn?"

"Well, I, uh . . ." It was the first time I'd ever seen Didra so rattled.

"Where do you want this?" I said to Didra, holding up the steak. Blood gathered in the corner of the plastic wrap. More blood.

"Give it to me." She tossed it into the refrigerator.

I reached into the bag for the last items. Two rolls of toilet paper. I smiled. That's one of the things I liked about Didra —even on a romantic weekend she remains practical.

"As I said, Didra," Griffin Coyle said, "you don't look much like your photo."

I guess I hadn't really heard him before, because it suddenly occurred to me: What photo? There weren't any in the cabin. My hand slapped my back pocket. Empty. I spun around, my hands balling to fists. "Where's my wallet, you son of a bitch?"

"Right here, Eric." He pulled it out of his own back pocket and handed it to me.

I opened it, counted the money. It was all there. The photo of Didra at last year's prom was still in the plastic pocket. She was wearing a tight coral-green gown that made her look like a mermaid.

The thing was, Griffin Coyle was right. Didra did look different now than she did in the photo. Not just in the way she was dressed or with her shorter hair, but in her face, her expression. She looked older, I guess, more focused. She always knew what she wanted, only now she looked as if she knew how to get it. I hadn't really noticed until now.

"You must have dropped it when you fell down outside," he said.

I tried to remember if I'd had it since then, tried to recall the feel of it when I sat down or moved around, the pressure of it against my body. I was almost certain that I'd felt it there when I'd been icing my knee. That means he'd have had to pick my pocket. But why go through all that trouble just to give it back without taking anything? Where was the logic? Just to look at my photos? Maybe he belonged to some kind of voodoo cult or Satan coven and he needed an object of mine to put a curse on me. Nothing seemed too weird for him.

"It's all there," he said, nodding at my wallet. "After all, I owe you one, Eric. And I never, never, never forget a debt. We're gonna be pals, you and me. You'll see." He looked me in the eye with such intensity that I looked away. Ashamed of my flinching, I looked back. He was smiling and rolling up his sleeves. "Now, how can I help with dinner? I'm not a bad cook, you know."

Neither of us answered him. We both stood and stared at his left wrist as he rolled the cuff higher and higher, each roll revealing more of the dark-blue portrait tattooed to the underside of his wrist. I felt a little like a Peeping Tom or something, peeking through someone's bedroom window. I didn't want to look, if for no other reason than I knew he wanted me to. But I couldn't turn away. Neither could Didra.

Not until we had seen the entire horrible, gruesome picture.

9

The first time I met Didra's parents was last summer. Didra invited me to the big Fourth of July cookout her dad threw every year. This was after my Hawaii trip, so I was still a little shaken up. Maybe she thought this would help.

"It'll be great," she'd promised. "Lots of food. Lots of drink. Lots of important people to make fun of."

"You're the only important person who'll be there," I'd said. I used to say stuff like that a lot. Not so much anymore. I learned it's best to save good lines like that for the right moment. That time I was rewarded with a long wet kiss.

"And bring your swimming suit so we can go in the pool."

"You have a pool?"

"Sure. And a Jacuzzi." She slid her hand along my thigh.

"How come you're inviting me to your house now? We've been seeing each other almost a year."

"Actually, it was Daddy's idea. He wants to meet you."

Now, I had never met Didra's folks before. She'd pointed them out at the play we were in, but we were peeking out at the audience from behind the wing curtains, and what with the glare from the stage lights, I wasn't positive which couple she was pointing at.

Even though I hadn't met them, I already had an attitude about them. I didn't like them. Part of that attitude came from my mom, who used to be a bit of a campus radical back in the '60s. She'd organized the boycott of television, hoping that the decrease in audience would force the sponsors to use their influence to end the Vietnam War. Lots of people signed the boycott pledges that Mom circulated around campuses, but she was constantly disappointed to catch them watching anyway. Once she tried to make Dad and me boycott the Super Bowl in an effort to stop apartheid in South America. Fortunately, Dad proved that such an action was ineffective and illogical. But both of us felt guilty the whole time we watched and ended up marching with Mom in an antiapartheid rally the next weekend in front of the White House. She doesn't do stuff like that anymore. Now she's into Buddhism and hopes to be declared the reincarnation of some ancient swami or something. But back when some of that old political activism was still in her, Dad and I used to hear Mr. Lester's name spoken often and with anger around the house whenever he appeared on TV or in the newspapers.

Mr. Lester had once been some sort of adviser to one of the presidents a few administrations ago. It was one of the administrations Mom didn't like, which doesn't rule out a whole lot. Now Mr. Lester had become a well-known and wealthy lobbyist, using his influence to get favorable legislation for his clients. Mom didn't like his clients, whom she described as "raping the land, exploiting the people, and undermining the Bill of Rights." Besides, he drove a Rolls-Royce.

Didra didn't talk about her parents much, but I got the distinct impression that they didn't approve of me going out with their daughter. I figured it was one of those wrong-side-of-the-tracks things, what with them owning most the money in the country and Dad just getting by on a professor's salary. I assumed they wanted their precious daughter hanging around with guys who came from wealthy families like theirs. Guys who, like Mr. Lester, went to Yale.

"Let's not go," I pleaded with Didra the day before the party. "Let's go someplace by ourselves. A drive."

"I can't, Eric. I have to be there."

"Why?"

"This is Daddy's Big Event. He invites all his clients and prospective clients. It's important to him to have his family there, you know, for his 'family man' image."

That's another thing. Even though Didra didn't talk about them much, whenever she did it was always in a sarcastic tone. That contributed to my not liking them without ever having met them.

I guess that's why I was so surprised when they greeted me at the door that Fourth of July.

"Mr. Marlowe," Westin Lester said with a huge smile. "I'm so glad you could make it. Deedee's spoken so highly of you. Come in, come in, young man."

We shook hands. He clasped both of his around mine and pumped vigorously.

"Oh, Eric," Mrs. Lester said, "Didra tells us you're quite the basketball star."

"Not really," I said.

"Such modesty is refreshing," Mr. Lester said, chuckling. He was a big man, bigger even than his photographs indicated. He was as tall as I was, but broader all the way around by sixty pounds. I figured him for about sixty-five, though he looked no more than fifty. He had two grown daughters in their thirties, who were married and lived in houses not more than a couple of miles away. Both husbands worked for Mr. Lester's firm. Didra had come late in his life.

Mrs. Lester stood in an elegant cream-colored pants and blouse outfit that showed off her slim figure. She was about forty, with soft blond hair like Didra's. She was not, however, the first Mrs. Lester, the mother to the two grown daughters. She had been a secretary at Mr. Lester's firm and married him shortly after his divorce. Eight months later Didra was born. "They tried to convince me I was premature," Didra once told me.

Mrs. Lester put her hand on my arm. Her fingernails were plum-colored and perfectly shaped, unlike Didra's unpainted chewed-to-the-nub fingernails. "We thought you were wonderful in that Shakespeare play. Very funny indeed. Wasn't he, Wes?"

Mr. Lester nodded. "The kid practically stole the show. You have a real flair for acting, Eric."

"Thank you, sir," I said.

Didra sat on one of the three sofas in the huge living room. She was behind them, so they couldn't see her. She made a goofy face at me and smiled.

"Well," I said. "I don't want to keep you from your guests." I could see about a hundred people milling about outside around the giant pool. Waitresses and waiters in white uniforms with silver trays circulated with drinks and food. The drinks all had sprigs of mint in them. The food was skewered with curly-headed toothpicks.

"Nonsense, Eric," Mr. Lester said with a laugh. "That's just business. This is personal. We've been looking forward to meeting you for a long time. I don't know why Deedee hasn't brought you over sooner."

I looked over at Didra. She didn't say anything. I was on my own.

The Lesters both sat down on opposite sofas. I was standing in the middle, so I sat down next to Didra. The fabric of the sofa was so smooth and silky I was afraid that just by sitting on it I would somehow damage it.

Mr. Lester pulled out a huge cigar and roasted the end of it while rolling it between his fingers. "Tell us about yourself, son."

A question like that drives me nuts. I mean, what exactly do they want to know? When I lost my baby teeth? Who was the first girl I kissed?

Mrs. Lester leaned forward. She was a knockout. They say if you want to know what a girl will look like twenty years from now, look at her mother, because that's what she will look like. If this was how Didra was going to look, I was very happy. "So, Eric," she said. "I suppose you'll be applying to colleges in a few months."

"Yes, ma'am."

"Ma'am? God, Wes, isn't that precious?"

"Do you know which schools you'll be applying to?" Mr. Lester asked.

"Not Yale," I said suddenly. It came out a little snottier than I'd wanted, but if they noticed, they didn't let on.

"Yale?" Mr. Lester said. "My goodness, why would a vibrant young man like yourself want to go there?" He made a sour face. "Awful place. Intellectual bores and rich kids strutting and fretting their hour upon the stage." He pointed his cigar at me. "Do you know what play that misquote comes from, Eric?"

"*Macbeth,* sir."

"Does it?" he said. "I'd forgotten. Well, now that we've eliminated Yale, where do you intend to matriculate?"

"I'll be attending the university. My father teaches there."

"Religion, isn't it?" Mr. Lester said through a cloud of gray smoke.

"Philosophy and logic."

"That's right." He sucked in another lungful. "Your mother lives in Hawaii now?"

"Yes, she does."

"Unfortunate," Mrs. Lester said.

"What are your plans, Eric?" Mr. Lester asked.

I wasn't sure what he meant exactly. Was he asking about my intentions toward Didra, what we'd be doing once we were alone, whether we planned to marry, buy a condo or lease an apartment?

"He means careerwise," Didra explained.

Mr. Lester nodded. "Yes. What do you plan to major in?"

"I haven't decided yet. My mother wants me to be a lawyer and sue everyone connected with toxic waste." I laughed until I realized that some of those same polluters were probably Mr. Lester's clients, outside right now sipping his minted drinks next to his Olympic-size pool. I stopped laughing.

But Mr. and Mrs. Lester laughed too. "That's a very noble cause, Eric. Your mother is quite right. Someone has to stop the madness, why not you?"

"Well, I haven't decided yet."

"What does your father advise?" he asked.

"He doesn't. He told me to take my time and do what I want."

Mr. Lester nodded. "A very enlightened man. Deedee tells me you write some."

I looked at Didra again, but she still wouldn't look back.

"Yes, sir. Ever since being in my first school play in junior high I've been jotting down scenes."

"Oh." Mrs. Lester clapped her hands together. "You're a playwright."

"Just scenes so far. Scribbles mostly."

Mr. Lester placed his cigar in an ashtray. The heavy smoke continued to curl lazily toward the ceiling. "Deedee here wants to be a journalist. A regular muckraker." He laughed. "Dig up the dirt and serve it up on a platter of newsprint. What do you think of that?"

"I think it's very exciting. Didra's very talented."

"Is she?" he said with a smile, as if he thought I was being amusing. "Have you read her writing?"

Actually, I hadn't. As editor of the newspaper, she was responsible for putting each issue together, but she never wrote any of the stories. In fact, I'd never read anything that she'd written herself. Funny, I'd never even thought about that before.

"She won't show any to us," Mrs. Lester said. "She can be so secretive."

Mr. Lester chuckled. "Deedee has dreams of exposing corruption. She sees juicy scandal everywhere. Don't you, sweetheart?"

"Can we go outside now," Didra said impatiently. "I'm hungry."

"Of course, darling." Mr. Lester stood up with remarkable grace for a man his size. He picked up his cigar and relit it. "I want you to be sure to introduce Mr. Marlowe here to everyone. Lots of powerful and influential people out there, Eric. Personally, I think they're a rather boring lot, but they have money, and you never know when an aspiring playwright might need some backers for his play."

"Well, I'm not really a playwright yet. I just dabble."

He reached into his pocket and pulled out a set of keys. He grinned, then tossed the keys to me. "You kids might want to take a little spin later. Why don't you take the Silver Cloud."

Jesus. The Rolls.

"Thank you, Mr. Lester."

He smiled, offered his arm to his wife, and escorted her out of the room. A thin tail of smoke lingered behind them.

I was stunned. I'd come here expecting some kind of classic showdown. The rich unscrupulous powerbroker grilling me, making me feel like creamed spinach. Maybe even offering to buy me off with a check, a job, anything I wanted if I would only stay away from his little girl. But they were nice. More than nice, they treated me like a welcome guest, as if they were glad I was dating Didra.

When they'd gone, I turned to Didra. "What was that all about?"

"What do you mean?"

"I don't know. They were so nice to me. As if they liked me."

"Of course they like you. What'd you expect?"

I bounced the keys to the Rolls-Royce in my palm. "Not this."

10 ≈

Griffin *Coyle handed us* each a plastic dinner plate filled with steaming food. "You're gonna love this. Trust me."

Didra and I were sitting at the kitchen table. Griffin had insisted we stay out of the way and let him do all the cooking and serving. "The least I can do after everything you've done for me."

"You still leave right after dinner," I reminded him. "That's the deal."

"Sure, Eric. I said I would, didn't I? Now eat." He sat down at the table with his own plate of food, but he didn't eat. He just watched us, waiting. "Go on, go on," he urged.

Didra went first. She cut a thin sliver of steak and stuck it in her mouth. She chewed slowly, as if she suspected there might be scrap metal hidden in the meat. After a couple of chews, she arched her eyebrows with surprise.

"Well, what do you think?" He had an anxious smile on his face.

"It's great," she said. I could tell she really meant it too. "Try it, Eric. It's better than I could have done."

Griffin shrugged modestly. "Just something I learned at the detention camp. I did a work rotation in the mess hall. They had a terrific cook, named Stash. A real honest-to-God Creole. Man, he could do things with potatoes you can't imagine. He cooked the way Pavarotti sings."

There he went again. I would have expected him to say "the way Phil Collins sings." Or Sting. Or Elvis. But never Pavarotti. I mean, how much opera do they listen to in prison? The only reason I knew about him was because Mom used to drag Dad and me to the opera every once in a while. She always cried during the performance. I always slept.

"Try it, Eric," he said. "It's not poisoned. Eric thinks I poisoned the food."

Didra nudged me. "Try it, Eric. It really is delicious."

I sliced off a small piece of my steak and forked it into my mouth. It was good, damn it.

"Eric's dad is a pretty good cook too," Didra said. "Isn't he, Eric?"

"I guess." I was willing to eat his food—after all, the punk did owe us that much—but I wasn't going to make polite dinner conversation with him. And, to tell you the truth, I was pretty annoyed at Didra for being so friendly.

"The steak was the easy part," Griffin said. "Just a matter of starting with a good piece of meat and a reliable broiler. Now, the vegetables, they were a challenge. Vegetables can break your heart." He said this with a straight face.

"They taste, I don't know, sweet, but a little bitter too." Didra took another forkful, smacking her lips, trying to figure out the taste.

"Just the right touch of this herb and that spice, that's my secret. And I'm taking it to the grave with me."

Didra laughed, which made me madder. I was sorry now I hadn't turned the bastard in when I'd had the chance. She cut another wedge of steak, a larger piece this time. I noticed that she had fingernail polish on, the same plum color that her mom wore. Also, her fingernails were not ragged from her constant chewing, they were perfectly shaped. This surprised me, because she used to make fun of her mother's constant attention to her fingernails.

Griffin smiled hugely, seemingly pleased with the way Didra was wolfing down his cooking. He pushed his sleeves up over his forearms and began to eat his own dinner. Once again, I stared across the table at his strange tattoo.

The lines were crudely drawn. Yet the detail was so thorough, done with such painstaking attention, I couldn't help but stare. It was a snarling beast with the head of an eagle and the body of a lion. Growing out of its ribs were long eagle wings that stood straight up as if preparing for flight. The creature's tail was a snake, which coiled along Griffin's wrist toward his hand. The snake's head reared back, its mouth gaping open, its fangs long and curved, as if it were about to strike someone sneaking up behind the creature. I remembered seeing this same beast in my mythology book from school. It was called a griffin.

The difference was that this griffin had a human heart clamped in its sharp beak and it was biting down hard enough to cause blood to drip from it. Three large drops of blood dotted Griffin's forearm.

"Would you like one?" Griffin asked.

"Huh?" I said, looking up.

"A tattoo. I did this one myself. I can do one for you. Not like this one, of course. This is my own personal statement."

"You did that yourself?" Didra asked. She sounded impressed.

"Yeah. You can always tell a prison tattoo from a commercial one." He ran his finger along the outline of the beak, but slowly, as if he were petting it. "See how rough the lines are? A professional uses a machine, like a portable sewing machine. The needle pecks at your skin like a crazy woodpecker while a steady flow of ink is pumped in. When you're in prison you use what you got. For instance, not everybody there is as artistically inclined as I am; they can't draw their own design. So they take some solid deodorant and rub it on the skin where they want the tattoo. Then they slap on the photo or drawing they snipped from some dumb biker or kung fu magazine with some carbon paper underneath and outline the sucker. When they take the page away, they got a perfect picture to work from. Oh yeah, and we don't have access to needles, so we have to use paper clips instead. We straighten them out and sharpen them against the floor. Then we unravel some thread from a shirt or pants and wrap it around the paper clip until just a tiny point sticks out, no bigger than a gnat's front tooth. The thread absorbs the ink, so it can be absorbed into your skin while you're getting jabbed."

Didra curled her lips in distaste. "Yeech."

"It gets worse," Griffin said. "Sometimes it's hard to get ink, so we have to burn the pages of a Bible and mix the ashes with toothpaste. And if we can't get any paper clips, we use staples from magazines. The real problem, though, is we can't sterilize anything, so there are all sorts of pus-filled infections you can get. Lots of times you end up with scars instead of tattoos."

"Sounds painful," Didra said, making a face. She put her fork and knife down.

"Hey, it's art. Everybody's gotta have some kind of art—music, drawing, something to keep your spirits up. But inside prison, man, it's not that easy. You hang a picture on the wall, somebody steals it. Or if the guards know you like the picture, they'll take it away as punishment. But with a tattoo, you got art no one can take away."

"I never thought of it like that before." Didra reached across the table and touched the tattoo, her plum-colored fingernails gliding across Griffin's skin.

Now, I'm not usually a jealous person, jealousy being an unreasonable emotion. But I could feel a prickly heat burning my skin. It was as if my whole face was getting a tattoo. I stabbed my fork into my steak as if it were Griffin's heart.

"It's amazing, isn't it, Eric?" Didra said, turning to me.

"What is? That he's got a tattoo? Lots of convicts have tattoos."

"No, that he did it himself."

I got up and went over to the kitchen phone. I took the pad of paper and pen from the counter and tossed them on the table next to Griffin's dinner plate. "Here," I said. "Draw that thing on this paper. I want to see how it would look on me."

Griffin looked up into my eyes. He seemed to see something there, because suddenly he grinned. "I don't think you believe I did this, Eric."

"There's an easy way to prove me wrong."

He picked up the pen and placed the tip against the pad. He stayed in that position about half a minute, without moving, before dropping the pen on the pad and pushing them away. "I think I'd rather eat right now. Maybe later, Eric, before I go."

"Yeah, right," I said. I sat back down feeling somehow triumphant, as if I'd just uncovered a fraud. But that feeling lasted only a moment, because neither Griffin nor Didra seemed affected by what had just happened. She continued to ask him questions about prison tattooing and other aspects of life there, and he answered each question with some story or other. Didra was in her reporter mode, interviewing him. It didn't seem to matter whether what he said was the truth or not.

I ate silently while the two of them chatted about prison life. There was no point in me making a big deal of it. As soon as dinner was over, Griffin Coyle and his tattoo would disappear from our lives forever.

When Griffin had swallowed his last bite, he pushed away from the table, thumped his stomach, and said, "Great meal, if I do say so myself."

"Why doesn't that surprise me," I said.

"Yeah, I guess maybe I am tooting my own horn, bro." He leaned back on two legs of his chair. "At the camp you gotta do a lot of posturing. To hear them tell it, everyone there is the baddest mutha in the world. Bragging is the official language."

"Sounds silly," Didra said.

"Out here it sounds silly. Sitting in your rich daddy's cabin munching steak it sounds silly. But inside it's a matter of survival. Inside there are two kinds of people, those who eat and those who get eaten. Everybody's busy trying to eat and still not get eaten. See what I mean? Like them blowfish. They start off as little fish swimming around. But at the first sign of danger, they puff themselves up so that they look bigger than they really are and scare bigger fish away. That's what happens in prison."

"I thought it was just a detention camp," Didra said. "Not a real prison."

He smiled without humor. "Whenever someone locks the door behind you, lady, it's a goddamn prison."

Embarrassed, Didra looked down at her plate. It was almost empty, but she pushed around a lone kernel of corn, finally spearing and eating it.

I felt bad too. My anger was stupid. He was just a kid, a kid who'd been locked away and was now on the run. Within a few minutes he and his tattoo and Tales from the Inside would be gone and none of this would matter anymore.

To hasten him on his way, I started clearing the dishes from the table. I took his first. I scraped the crumbs and steak bones into the trash and rinsed the dishes. I figured we could wash them in the morning. Right now I just wanted him out of here so that I could finally be alone with Didra.

"Better do them dishes right away, Eric," Griffin said. "You let 'em sit overnight and you'll wake up to a billion ants crawling across your kitchen."

"We'll do them later," I said, looking at him so that he got my meaning.

"Fine. But in the morning you'll come out here and find them carrying your furniture down the driveway." He turned to Didra. "Can I bum a smoke from you, Deedee?"

"She doesn't smoke," I said.

"Sure she does, Eric."

"No, she doesn't." Not smoking was one of the things Didra and I had in common from the start. "Tell him, Didra."

Didra didn't say anything. She was twisting the drain cover into place and filling the sink with hot water. She squirted some Joy into the water and it started bubbling.

"Didra," I said.

"Oh, what's the big deal?" she said, throwing up her hands. She shut off the water, marched to her purse, and dug out a pack of cigarettes. She tossed the pack on the kitchen table. Salem menthol.

Griffin grinned at me as he reached for the pack, shook a

cigarette loose, and screwed it into the corner of his mouth. He leaned back on two legs of his chair until he was close to the stove. He turned on the burner flame, leaned the cigarette into the fire, and puffed away. "Like the Beatles said, Eric, 'Everybody's got somethin' to hide, 'cept me and my monkey.'"

I was stunned. Didra and I had often waited extra time at restaurants to sit in the nonsmoking section. She used to point to women smoking and tell me how ridiculous they looked sucking on a cigarette. We talked about how unhealthy it was for everyone around, how it polluted the air. Not smoking wasn't just avoiding a bad habit, it was embracing a philosophy of lifestyle we both shared. Same with not taking drugs.

"Don't look at me like that," Didra said to me. "Like I shot your puppy. I only do it once in a while. When I study for exams. It relaxes me."

I didn't say anything. I dunked the dishes into the soapy water and began washing them. I realized it wasn't the smoking that bothered me. It was that Didra had a secret. I didn't have any secrets. It made me feel alone.

"I knew you wouldn't understand," she said. "That's why I didn't tell you."

"It's okay," I said. "You just caught me by surprise. No big deal."

I scrubbed the aluminum skillet that Griffin had cooked the vegetables in. I could see his reflection in the pan; he was leaning back in his chair smoking Didra's cigarette. The smile on his face was exaggerated by the curve of the pan. I wondered how he knew she smoked, and I didn't. The same way he'd noticed how different she looked from the photograph and I hadn't.

"College is not like high school," Didra went on. "In high

school it was easy to get good grades. But college is different. *Everybody* at this school is smart. The pressure is tremendous. So, okay, I started to smoke a little during exams. It's not that big of a deal."

"It's okay," I said, trying to sound as if I meant it.

"Jesus!" She grabbed the pack from the table and walked over to the grocery bag we were using for trash. She threw the pack into the garbage. "Okay? Satisfied?"

Griffin said, "If you're going to throw them away anyway, mind if I have them? Eric?"

Angrily, I dropped the frying pan into the water. It splashed sudsy water up over the counter. Some splashed onto my shirt and pants. Some spilled onto the floor. I spun around to Didra and said, "I don't care if you smoke." Then to Griffin, "I don't care if you root through the trash." And to both of them, "Everybody has my blessing to do whatever the hell they want. Okay?"

A car crunched gravel and dirt outside. Sounded like someone chewing granola. It was dark outside and the car's headlights washed through the cabin. The three of us froze in place as if we'd been caught in the middle of a burglary. We listened to the car door slam, the scrape of footsteps. Three loud raps on the front door.

"Hello inside." Three more raps. "This is Sheriff Jim Forrest."

Griffin grabbed a steak knife from the dishes I'd just washed.

11

Griffin *hunched in the middle* of the kitchen clutching his steak knife, waving it back and forth as if unsure which of us to attack first. Gone was his usual smug grin, the cocky expression. His mouth was twisted into a thin snarl. His eyes glowed bright and feverish. The transformation was so sudden it was like watching those antidrug films in school in which some wimpy kid smokes some PCP and two seconds later he's ripping the engine out of his parents' Oldsmobile.

Standing there, wielding that knife, Griffin looked completely out of place in a kitchen, under bright lights, surrounded by modern appliances. Instead I pictured him dressed in animal hides, chucking a crude wooden spear into some scampering animal. Then I saw him falling to the ground, his bared teeth tearing into its still-warm corpse, eating the creature raw, its guts and blood staining his greasy beard. The gaping red wound over his brow only enhanced that caveman image.

"Put that knife away," Didra whispered urgently.

He pivoted toward her so quickly that I thought he was going to stab her. I took a step toward him and he swung back toward me. He never actually threatened us with the knife, but I somehow knew he'd use it if he had to.

"Easy, man," I said, holding up my hands, backing away.

"What's *he* doing here?" Griffin rasped.

"I don't know."

The loud knocking continued. "Anybody home?"

"He can see our lights," Didra said. "He knows we're here."

"Are you gonna tell him?" Griffin asked. "You gonna tell him about me?"

There was something touching in the way he asked, like a child afraid of being tattled on about breaking a cheap lamp. However, I reminded myself that he had probably not been arrested for breaking a lamp. That he was an escaped criminal. That he was holding a knife on us.

"We won't tell," Didra promised.

Griffin looked at me.

I didn't say anything.

Three more hard raps rattled the front door. "Someone doesn't answer this door, I'm going to have to bust in there."

"C'mon," Didra said, taking my hand. She and I pushed through the swinging kitchen door and walked straight to the front door. She opened it.

Sheriff/Reverend Jim Forrest stood in the doorway. He wore the same jeans and khaki shirt I'd seen him in earlier. They were a lot muddier now though, and a button was missing at the stomach. The shirt bloused out where the button was missing and I could see hard stomach muscles beneath the khaki fabric. His shirtsleeves were rolled up much the same way that Griffin's were and I noticed that his forearms were knotted with sinewy muscle and ropy veins. He nodded recognition at me. "Hello, son."

"Hi, Sheriff," I said.

"Sheriff?" Didra said. "I don't see any badge."

"Oh, yeah," he said, chuckling in a friendly way. He patted all his pockets before finally digging a silver badge out of his jeans. He showed the badge to Didra. "You D.C. folks like all the formalities."

"When it comes to someone knocking on our door in the middle of the night we do," Didra said. She'd been around enough powerful people in Washington to not be intimidated by this hick sheriff. She looked the badge over carefully as if she knew just what to look for in a forgery.

"I don't blame you for being careful. Smart thing to do, ask for ID." He slipped the badge back into his pocket. "Of course, these babies aren't that hard to come by, so the best thing to do is to keep your door locked until you've checked the ID through your peephole. Then phone the sheriff's office and ask for a description of the man by badge number. Only then should you open your door. Well, too late for all that now. I'm already in." And he took a couple steps into the living room. He glanced over at the fire in the fireplace.

"What can we do for you, Sheriff?" Didra asked.

The firelight caught the curled scar on his cheek and made it look wet and slippery.

"Still looking for that kid who escaped from Wise Acres."

"Wise Acres?" I asked.

"That's the name of the juvey detention camp down the road. Man who started it was a retired high school principal. Ken Bannon. Ken had the idea that all troubled kids needed was some time to put their thoughts together. So along with the formal schooling the law mandated, he'd teach them farming. He thought learning about the land would help kids learn about themselves. I heard him say more than once that if you let kids dig in the dirt deep enough, they're bound to find themselves. Like some sort of buried treasure, I guess. Some folks thought he was too soft or too corny." The sheriff paused a moment as if considering that possibility. "Doesn't much matter now. He died a few years ago and the new guy who runs that place has a whole different approach. Hard time." He smiled, giving no indication which approach he favored.

I thought I heard a faint sound in the kitchen.

The sheriff peered over my shoulder toward the kitchen door. "You hear that?"

"What?" Didra said. I looked at Didra, but I couldn't tell if she was lying. She can look so innocent sometimes.

The sheriff looked at me. "You hear anything?"

"Yes. I think we've got some mice. I chased one out of the kitchen before Didra got here. I didn't want to tell her."

"Mice?" Didra said, grimacing. "Ugh."

The sheriff stared at me, then Didra, then back at me. I couldn't tell whether or not he was buying our little act. Finally he nodded and said, "You get a nest of field mice in here and they can be tough to get rid of. You have to trap them."

"We'll manage," Didra said. Her tone added the unspoken, *Thanks for dropping by, now get the hell out of here.*

If Sheriff Forrest picked up on her subliminal message, he ignored it. "Anyway," he continued, "someone thought they saw the kid who escaped heading this way. Since your cabin is usually unoccupied this time of year, I thought Griffin might hole up here awhile."

"We haven't seen anyone," Didra said. "What's he look like?"

"Can't miss him. He's got red hair and a funny tattoo on

his arm. Right here." He touched his own forearm, his fingernail tracing the mythological beast on his bare skin. The
ghostly outline remained etched on his skin a couple seconds
before fading. "The camp discourages that sort of thing, tattooing. But you can't watch them all the time, can you?" He
paused as if waiting for an answer.

"What did he do, Sheriff?" I asked.

"Oh, this 'n' that. Always been in trouble."

"But what was he sentenced to Wise Acres for?"

The sheriff's face hardened. "Selling drugs. Crack co-
caine."

I glanced at Didra. She looked back with a confused
expression. We hadn't considered his crime to be that serious. He'd said something to us about destroying public property. I figured maybe he'd smashed some parking meters or
something, the way Paul Newman had in *Cool Hand Luke*. I
thought of him out in the kitchen, the steak knife in his fist,
the wild look in his eyes. I didn't know what to do. Griffin
Coyle had lied to us, so we weren't bound by any promise
not to turn him over to the sheriff. In fact, *I'd* never promised
him anything. Didra had.

"And he beat a guy," the sheriff continued. "Another kid
at the camp. Worked him over pretty badly. Put him in the
infirmary. That'll add some time to his sentence."

I thought about the steak knife. The ozone layer. My
stolen wallet. The tattoo. Dinner. The bullet scar. Didra's
cigarettes.

Sheriff Forrest walked over to the fire and stuck his
hands out as if to warm them. "Nice fire. You build it, son?"

"Yes, sir," I lied.

"Did it just right. Country style. The way we do it around
here."

"I showed him how," Didra piped in. "My dad taught me."

"Well, your daddy's been coming down here enough years, I guess he ought to have picked up a few local customs." He walked around the room, staring at the things on the wall, the expensive prints, the bookshelves crowded with biographies of Iacocca, Eisenhower, Nixon, some Japanese book called *The Art of War.* He continued down the hall to the bedroom and the bathroom, peeking in, poking here and there with a finger, a foot.

"Don't you need a search warrant in this county, Sheriff?" Didra asked.

"I'm not searching, young lady. Just running a security check, making sure your windows are secured properly." He smiled at her. "They are."

Didra rolled her eyes at me.

When we returned to the living room, Sheriff Forrest nodded admiringly. "Lovely cabin. Nicer than most folks' regular homes."

"I'll tell Daddy you said so," Didra said. There was a hint of threat in her voice.

The sheriff turned around and smiled at her. "Oh? Your daddy know you two are down here? Alone?"

"Is that any business of the sheriff's office?"

His smile broadened. "I'm not speaking as the sheriff now, young lady. I only do that part-time. We don't have enough crime to justify a full-time sheriff. No, I'm speaking now as a reverend. Full-time reverend."

"I see," Didra said. "You may not have enough crime for a full-time sheriff, but we have enough sin for a full-time reverend?"

He chuckled. "You're very clever. I hope you're not going

to ask me to pull out a clerical collar, because I don't wear one."

I moved close to the fire and felt the flames toast my face. I was still trying to decide what to do about Griffin, to rat him out or not. Here I was again with the ball in my hands, the clock ticking off seconds so loudly I couldn't hear anything else, the hoop hanging twenty feet in the air and only big enough around for a tennis ball to squeeze through, the crowd shouting in unison with the ticking clock, "Shoot! Shoot! Shoot!" If I shoot, the ball cannot physically fit through the hoop; if I don't shoot, we'll lose the game by one point. *"Shoot! Shoot! Shoot!"*

Sheriff/Reverend Forrest started toward the front door. "Well, guess I've done my duty in warning you kids. Say, what happened to your car? Looks pretty banged up."

"Got a flat tire," I said. "Spun it out of control on the dirt and gravel."

He nodded. "I'll send Bobby Hodges, have him come out tomorrow with his tow truck. See if he can fix it."

"Thanks," I said.

"Don't expect too much from Bobby. He does lousy body work, but he'll get it running well enough to get you back to D.C."

"Thank you, Sheriff," Didra said. She escorted him to the door.

He reached out, grabbed the doorknob. He stopped suddenly. "You know, I sure could use a drink of water before I head home. Hunting Griffin is thirsty work."

Without waiting for a word from us, he marched straight for the kitchen, with Didra and I chasing after him.

He pushed open the door to the kitchen. "Well, well," he said. "Well, well."

12 ⁀

"No wonder," Sheriff/Reverend Forrest said.

Didra and I ran into the kitchen behind him expecting to see Griffin launching himself at the sheriff, plunging his steak knife into the man's chest.

No one was there.

"No wonder you've got mice," he said, pointing at the grocery bag filled with garbage from dinner. "You leave your trash open like this, that's like an engraved invitation. You'd better dump that bag or by morning this whole cabin will be crawling with ants."

I looked in the trash bag. Oddly, it was almost full. When I'd scraped the steak bones into the bag a few minutes ago, it had only been a quarter full. The steak bones and Didra's cigarettes were still on top, so whatever had filled up the bag was buried underneath.

The kitchen was too small for many hiding places. And

the back door was still padlocked from the inside. There was only one window, a greenhouse window over the sink, crammed with small pots of dead plants. The window could be cranked open, but not far enough for anyone to squeeze through. Where the hell was he? I could tell by Didra's face that she was wondering the same thing.

I glanced at the cupboard under the sink. Maybe . . .

Sheriff Forrest walked over to the sink, took one of the glasses from the drain board, ran the water, tested the temperature with his finger, and ducked the glass under the faucet. He drank, his eyes roving around the kitchen. When he finished, he rinsed the glass off and returned it to the drain board, upside down. He squatted beside the sink. "You know, sometimes those mice like to nest right here. They like the dark." He yanked open both cupboard doors.

I thought I heard Didra gasp, though it might have been the cupboard hinges squeaking.

The sheriff stared into the cupboard. A can of Raid Ant & Roach Killer. A can of Drāno. A box of Brillo pads. A box of hundred-watt lightbulbs. A flashlight. Five or six batteries.

No Griffin.

He closed the cupboard and stood up. I couldn't tell if he'd expected to find anything else, or if he was disappointed. He was smiling. "No mice there."

We followed him back to the front door. This time he went through it. He paused on the porch, turned, and looked me right in the eye. It was that same look that Griffin had given me earlier, the one that suggested he knew my secrets. I had the feeling that he was giving me one more chance to tell him the truth about Griffin.

I didn't. But this time it wasn't like when I let the cab driver go. This time I knew why I didn't speak, why I didn't inform him I was hiding a violent escaped convict brandishing a steak knife.

Because, finally, I too knew what it felt like to have secrets.

13 ≈

After we heard the sheriff's Jeep drive away, Didra and I ran for the kitchen.

"Where is he?" she asked as we burst into the kitchen.

"I don't know. I don't know."

Didra dropped to her knees and pulled open the cupboards under the sink again. Nothing had changed there. Same cans. Same boxes. No Griffin.

I went to the trash bag and rooted through the steak bones, cucumber peels, plastic wrap, Styrofoam tray, empty tin cans. Suddenly my fingertips brushed something cold. I grabbed it and yanked it up through the garbage. A full jar of applesauce. I distinctly remembered putting that in the refrigerator when Didra and I unpacked.

"Look at this," I said.

Didra climbed off her knees. "Yeah, so? It's applesauce."

"I got it out of the trash."

We exchanged puzzled expressions. Then it hit us both at

the same time. I turned and yanked open the door of the refrigerator.

The food and metal shelves had all been removed. Crunched into the refrigerator, his legs and arms pretzeled grotesquely like some kind of rubber man, Griffin hid. The steak knife was still firmly clenched in his shivering hand.

Didra reached in and grabbed an arm. Carefully she untwisted his limbs. He climbed out on his own, rubbed his hands briskly, and coughed. "Boy, now I know how a side of beef feels."

His skin was pale, his lips blue. But he was smiling again, grinning like he owned the world. It made me wish I'd turned him in.

"I'll make some hot tea," Didra said. She filled a pot with water and put it on the stove.

I started digging out the food he'd dumped into the trash, rinsing it off, and returning it to the refrigerator.

"The racks are behind the stove," he said. He sat at the kitchen table and clamped his hands over his ears, trying to warm them.

I slid the racks back in and finished storing the food. Didra fussed with selecting the right tea bag from about ten different kinds. Her parents drank only tea since they spent a summer in England a few years ago.

No one said anything for a long time.

Finally Griffin broke the silence. "I wasn't sure I'd fit," he said cheerfully. "But I knew he'd find some excuse to check out the kitchen. He did come out here, didn't he?"

"Yes," Didra said. "For a glass of water."

"I knew he would. But I foxed him. I foxed the bastard." He tugged on his fingers, working the blood back into circulation. "Thing is, you can't hear anything in there. I wasn't sure if he'd left already or if he was standing right next to me.

I figured I'd better play it safe and wait until one of you realized where I was." The tattoo on his forearm looked somehow darker. Maybe it was just that the cold had made his skin paler.

"You lied to us," I said.

"When?"

"You told us you were in that camp because you destroyed some public property."

"That's right."

Didra set the cup of steaming tea in front of him. She backed away and stood next to me.

"The sheriff told us you were in for selling drugs."

There was a pause while Griffin sipped his tea. He set the cup down and looked up at us. "Got any honey? I'll settle for sugar, but I'd prefer honey."

I grabbed the sugar bowl from the counter and slammed it down on the table next to his cup. Tea slurped over the rim of his cup into the saucer. He methodically lifted the cup and poured the tea back in. Then he added three teaspoons of sugar and slowly stirred, the spoon rattling the cup with each stir.

"If you thought I lied, why didn't you turn me in?" he asked quietly.

Didra and I looked at each other, as if we hoped the other would be able to answer for both of us. Actually, now that I thought about it, why didn't Didra turn him in? She wasn't the overly sentimental type who took in stray dogs and tended birds with broken wings. Not that she'd avoid doing it, she just didn't go out of her way to seek the helpless out. Neither did I. Why didn't she turn him in?

"I didn't lie to you," he said. "I told you I was in that camp for destroying public property. That's true. I stole the sheriff's Jeep, filled it with horse manure from Jimmy

Danton's farm, and set the whole thing on fire in front of city hall. Man, you shoulda seen it. It was fantastic." His face lit up as if he were reliving that moment of triumph, the flames lighting up his face. "You could see it for miles. Even better, you could smell it for days." He laughed.

"What about the drug charges?" Didra asked.

"Bullshit charges. They couldn't prove I'd torched the Jeep, so they framed me on the drug charges. That's the way justice works around here. Once they've got it in for you, you're finished."

"If that's true," Didra asked, "why'd you steal the Jeep in the first place?"

Griffin's face drooped into a grim scowl. He shrugged. "Kicks, I guess. What's the difference?" He sipped his tea.

"You know," I said, "he didn't seem like such a bad guy."

Griffin laughed bitterly. "Scarface? Yeah, he's a prince." He smirked at me. "You're a shrewd judge of character, aren't you, dude?"

That was enough. Whatever reasons I'd had for protecting him up to now, they were cancelled. When I spoke, I tried to keep my voice level, logical. "You've had your dinner, you've had your tea. We didn't tell anyone about your being here."

"Thou shalt be rewarded, brother, in a place greater than this." He waved his hands with evangelical fervor. "Can I have an amen?"

"I think it's time you moved on." I crossed my arms and gave him the big staredown that I used to use on my opponents in wrestling. I didn't want to provoke a fight—after all, the sheriff told us he'd put some guy in the infirmary—but neither was I willing to endure any more of his wiseass behavior. "Take some food with you, but go. Now."

He nodded his head. He finished his tea, set the cup back

on the saucer, and stood up. He hitched his pants. "Guess I've overstayed my welcome, huh? You two probably want to be alone. Am I right? Sure. That's why you came here, right?" He pushed the chair back into place at the table. He placed the spoon in the empty cup. "Thanks for what you've done, both of you. I appreciate it."

We followed him through the kitchen door. I put my arm around Didra's waist and she automatically folded against my body, hip to hip.

At the front door, Griffin unfurled his sleeves, covering his tattoo. He buttoned each cuff. He also buttoned the front of his shirt all the way up to the throat. "Gets cold out there at night," he explained. He opened the front door, started to walk through, then stopped. He turned and smiled at Didra. "Would've made a hell of a story, wouldn't it? I mean, you being a journalism student and all. About the corruption down here, how they railroaded an innocent kid. Hell of a story, I bet."

"So long," I said, as a way to urge him along.

"Yeah. So long." He offered his hand to me. "Almost blood brother."

This good-bye was taking longer than the fall of Rome. Just to get it over with, I shook his hand.

"Hell of a story." He grinned. "Am I right?"

He walked out of the cabin and down the steps.

"Wait," Didra said.

Griffin stopped. When he turned back he was smiling, as if he'd expected her to stop him.

"Can you back up your story with verifiable facts? Proof?"

He shrugged. "I can tell you my story. Digging up proof is your job, isn't it?"

"Didra," I said. "You can't trust this guy, he's a born liar."

"I know that. But if even half of what he says is true, I've got a great story."

Griffin walked back up the stairs and stood in the doorway. "Tell you what. You folks let me spend the night, just sleep here until morning, and I'll tell you the whole story. The whole truth, nothing but the truth, so help me God."

Didra turned to me. Her face was flushed with excitement. "Eric, this could be a big break for me. A chance to show what I can do. Something other than interviewing some college professor about his recent paper on the habits of anteaters during mating season. This could be important."

"What're you talking about? This guy is a hood."

Griffin laughed. "Just what are the habits of anteaters during mating season?"

"Shut up," I snapped at him. To Didra I said, "We haven't seen each other in three months. We've been planning this weekend together since August. Just the two of us."

Didra grabbed my wrists. It was an odd gesture, reminding me of my days as a wrestler. "Just one night. I'll interview him, maybe get some dirt on the way the local authorities operate. Jesus, Eric, we're talking about maybe *60 Minutes* or *20/20*. My story going national. This is just the kind of juicy little rat's hole they like to expose."

"That's true, Eric," Griffin said. "Send Mike Wallace and a camera crew over to Jim Forrest, see just what he's made of."

I turned toward Griffin. He had one foot on the porch steps, ready to climb back into our lives. "How did you know Didra was studying journalism?" I asked him.

"You musta said something during dinner, I guess."

"No, we didn't. I specifically avoided giving you any information about her."

"Well, then I don't know. Let me think. . . ." He scratched his head.

"Didra, did you bring your school books?"

"Yes," she said. "A few. In my briefcase in the bedroom."

"When he was in the living room making the fire, he sneaked into the bedroom and looked through your briefcase. That's the only way he would know."

Didra's eyes flared. She spun toward Griffin. "You son of a bitch!"

Griffin only smiled. "Well, yes, ma'am, that's true enough. I am a son of a bitch. If I weren't, I wouldn't be very valuable to you, now would I?"

"Get out of here," I said. "Get out."

Griffin's face hardened. In the darkness, his red hair looked black. The wound slicing his forehead looked black too. I could tell from his expression that he wanted to run up those steps and start swinging at me. I was hoping he wouldn't do that, because I wasn't so sure I could take him, and if I couldn't, where did that leave Didra? But I figured it would be a mistake to show any weakness, so I took a step toward him, lowering one foot to the porch step.

He seemed to find this amusing and cracked a little smile. He turned and walked away without a word. My knees wobbled with relief.

Until Didra ran after him.

"Wait, Griffin," she called. Her Reeboks spanked the dirt road.

He didn't stop.

"Damn it, Didra," I said and ran after her.

When she caught up to him, she grabbed his wrists the same way she had grabbed mine, in the odd wrestler's stance. She huffed, trying to speak and catch her breath at the same time. "Okay. One night. Exclusive interview. You leave at first light. That's the deal."

"I don't know," he said, shaking his head.

"Don't try to work me, kid. That's the deal, period. You wanna play games, fine." Didra marched away from him. By then I'd caught up and started walking beside her.

"What did you do that for?" I said.

"It's just business," she said. "When an opportunity comes along, a good journalist has to be able to recognize, then exploit it."

"Who's exploiting whom?"

She smiled at me. "I know what I'm doing, Eric."

"Hey, wait up," Griffin called. "You got yourself a deal."

14 ～

"Right about there," Didra said, pointing. "No, to the left."

"Here?" I said.

"Yes. The lighting's crucial."

I set the lamp down, plugged it in, and turned it on. It had a three-way bulb, which I cranked up to 150 watts. Didra studied the setup for a few seconds, her plum-colored fingernails fidgeting against her lips. A couple of months ago she'd have chewed them into stubs by now.

"More light," she decided. "We need a few more lamps."

I'd already crowded four lamps together, but I went scavenging through the cabin again and returned with a couple more. She directed me where to set them up.

Did you ever get a feeling you were caught in something doomed and even though you knew it was going to turn out badly for everyone, there was nothing you could do to stop it? Like in those movies where the hero is going down some steep mountain road and his brakes give out. He can't stop the car and it keeps going faster and faster. He wrestles with the steering wheel to keep the car from either crashing into the mountain on one side or plunging over the cliff on the other side. But the car keeps picking up speed and soon we know that even he won't be able to keep it under control and it will smash into the mountain or hurtle over the cliff. Fortunately, there's usually some kind of road construction going on with a big pile of dirt handy so he can steer the car into the soft dirt. The hero then climbs out unhurt and says something witty like, "This sort of thing always happens after I wash my car."

But piles of soft dirt are hard to come by when you really need them. And we were picking up speed.

"This is good. This will work." Didra was busy adjusting lamp shades so that they threw the proper light on the two chairs she'd placed in the middle of the living room. She turned to me. "Did you find that extension cord?"

"Yes," I answered. I'd taken it from the TV in the bedroom.

"Okay, good. Just hook it up to that ceramic lamp there and move it over by the sofa."

While I moved the ceramic lamp, Didra sat in one of the chairs and fussed with the videocamera she'd gotten out of the bedroom closet. It was the family vacation camera, just for shooting the family while they stayed here. Didra said they had ones just like it at their other two vacation homes. She pressed a button and the tape in the camera began to rewind.

"There might be something on that tape," I said.

"There is. Me and Daddy playing tetherball in the back. Boring stuff."

"Not to your folks."

Didra set the camera in her lap and looked up at me. She lowered her voice, even though Griffin was in the bathroom taking a bath. He'd refused to be photographed without washing up first. He'd been in there almost an hour now. "Eric, whose side are you on?"

"What are my choices?"

"Very funny."

"I'm on your side. You know that."

"You're not acting like it. Ever since I decided to do this interview, you've been really negative about it."

"I just don't trust him. He's a liar and a thief, we know that much for sure. He may be even worse."

"If he were an angel, there'd be no point to all this, would there?" That was almost exactly what Griffin had said earlier. It annoyed me even more that now she was quoting him.

Didra aimed the camera at me and put her eye to the eyepiece. She squinted the other eye closed. "Testing light and sound levels. Testing, testing, testing." She lowered the camera, adjusted a knob or two. She looked very professional sitting there fooling with the camera. The lamps, too, though makeshift, looked professional. We're talking about a very bright girl here, but one who never took a photograph in her life without blurring it. How had she learned all this technical Hollywood stuff in three months?

I sat down in the chair next to her. "I missed you, that's all."

She stopped adjusting the camera, put it on the floor, and leaned over and kissed me. It was a long, lingering kiss, with lips mashed tight, tongues sliding against each other. It was the kind of kiss I'd been waiting three months for. We had written at least once a week, and talked on the phone every Sunday night at six before *60 Minutes,* which she never missed. But there is nothing like the touch of another person, her smell, the way her head fits just so against yours. As individual as fingerprints. My heart was thumping, my skin tingling.

She pulled back slowly. "I've missed you, too, sweetheart. I really have."

"Then can we get this thing over with and still salvage some time for ourselves?"

"Just give me an hour. One hour, I promise."

I held up my index finger. "One hour. Then you and I adjourn to a separate room."

"Agreed. Shake." She put out her hand and I shook it. She laughed. We kissed again.

"Well, how do I look?" Griffin said.

Didra and I broke our kiss to look at him. "Jesus," I said, wincing.

"My God!" Didra gasped.

He wore the same tattered clothes, denim pants and blue shirt with almost my locker number stenciled on the pocket. But the dirt and grime were scrubbed off his face and his skin shone. His long red hair was still wet, combed straight back like a gangster's. He looked older now, a little like those *GQ* magazine models that stand around laughing their asses off because they're wearing certain brands of clothing that no one else can afford. That's not what shocked us though. It was his wound, the four-inch gash in his forehead. He had sewn it closed with black thread. The holes where he'd jabbed the needle through were pinpoints of bright red blood. A long black thread dangled down from one end of the seam all the way to his jaw. "How do ya like it?" he said cheerfully. "I did it myself. Found a little sewing kit in the bedroom dresser."

"You did that *yourself*?" Didra asked. She made a queasy face.

"Yeah, sure. Just like sewing up torn pants. My mother taught me how to sew when I was a kid. Nothing to it." He lifted the loose end of thread and walked toward us. "I could use a hand tying it off, though."

Didra recoiled as if he were holding out a hissing snake. She backed up a couple steps.

"It won't bite you, for chrissake. You just tie a couple knots, that's all. Like a button."

The spiral stitching looked fairly professional, even if the black thread looked sinister, like a pirate's scar or something. I was pretty certain that I'd never have had the nerve to sew up my own face like that. I had to admit, I was impressed.

"I'll do it," I said.

He smiled at me and I had the sudden feeling that that's what he'd wanted all along.

"What'll I do?" I said.

He handed me a sewing needle that was bent into a slight curve. "Thread the needle."

I did.

"Okay, now, you need to do one more stitch through the skin."

"What for? It looks closed enough to me."

"Just do it, okay? How many cuts you sewn up before, bro?"

I pinched the needle between thumb and forefinger. Slowly, I nudged the point of the needle against his skin. The wound was like a mouth and I was at the very corner of the lips.

"Come on, come on," he urged impatiently. "You're holding up my television debut. You can do it, can't you? I mean, you're not gonna faint or nothing?"

I jabbed the needle through the skin. Blood seeped around the silver needle. I tasted something metallic in my mouth. I poked the needle the rest of the way through both sides of the wound and pulled it taut. The black thread followed the needle, cinching the wound closed.

"Now, tie it off on the other thread. Just like a button. You know how to sew on a button, for chrissake, don't ya?"

I didn't answer. I concentrated on tying the knots. Actually, I knew how to sew fairly well. My dad taught me years ago. Mom could sew, but she never seemed to get around to it, what with her teaching and her paintings. She always insisted that we leave the sewing for her on the sewing machine, but months would go by and the same buttonless shirts or unhemmed pants would still be there long after the seasons had changed. So Dad and I took to sneaking in and sewing a shirt or two ourselves. We always left something behind though, because he said Mom wanted to feel as if we needed her. That it didn't matter if she actually finished the sewing, just as long as she knew we needed her to do it. It was complex logic, but it turned out Dad was right, because every once in a while Mom would ask us for anything we needed sewn, saying she was going to sew that week. So Dad and I would rip off a button or two from shirts we didn't wear often, and give them to her. She would smile happily and sit down and start sewing. But after about half an hour, she'd get an idea about some art piece she wanted to do and she'd be gone into her studio in the garage. Then Dad and I would sneak the shirts back and sew on the buttons again.

"There," I said, stepping back to admire my work. Not bad. "I thought you didn't care about scars," I said, remembering Walter, the bullet scar he'd showed me.

"Hey, I didn't want to look like some beaten-up loser on national television."

"Why'd you use black thread? You look like Frankenstein's monster."

"I figured the black thread would show up better on camera, make me more sympathetic to the audience."

"I thought the truth was supposed to do that," I said.

Griffin snorted. "Maybe in Oz, where you obviously come from. But in the real world, the truth is just another product on an overcrowded shelf that needs proper packaging. If you don't market it properly, nobody buys it. So what good does the truth do you if nobody buys it? Just ask your girlfriend. I'm sure she's learned that much at her fancy college. Am I right?"

Didra gestured to the chair next to her. "Sit here, please." Griffin did so. Didra handed me the camera. "Just screw it into the tripod and point it at Griffin. We'll keep it pointed at him the whole time. When we're done, you can shoot a few reverse angle shots that I'll edit in later."

"Reverse angle?" I asked.

Griffin laughed. "You know, that's when they show the reporter asking questions or nodding at certain answers. They shoot those after the interview is over. You didn't know that?"

"Of course I knew that," I said. "I just didn't know what it was called. Technically."

I set the camera up and focused it on Griffin. He looked different through the camera lens, more mature, relaxed, somehow friendlier. His smirk came across as a warm smile, his calculating eyes were softened to sincerity. Somehow the camera translated his image into something much more appealing. And he was right about the black thread, it did make him look more sympathetic through the camera.

"Got him," I said.

Didra cleared her throat and picked up the pad with a few questions she'd jotted down. "Okay, Eric, start the camera."

I did. The faint whirr of the tape droned next to my ear. Didra asked questions, Griffin answered. He spoke very convincingly. I didn't actually bother to listen to him, since I knew he was a liar. I was more fascinated with his image in the camera. His face was a model of the innocent victim persecuted by powerful, corrupt forces. It was like watching a play on television. Every once in a while I'd look up from the camera to make sure he was really the one I was taping. The same guy who'd stolen and wrecked my dad's car, lifted my wallet, burglarized the cabin as well as Didra's briefcase, maybe sold drugs, maybe set fire to the sheriff's Jeep, maybe beat some guy until he needed to be hospitalized. The truth was a slippery commodity around Griffin. Who knew for sure what really happened?

"The Pegs work their asses off all day—"

"The 'Pegs'?" Didra asked.

"Yeah, the Pegs. That's what we call the kids locked up inside, what we call each other. Pegs. We call the camp itself the Square. It's like they're trying to jam us round pegs into their square hole and we just don't fit, man. It ain't an easy fit. I mean, somethin's gotta give, right?"

Griffin's voice was different from when he spoke to us. His tone was gruffer, he used more slang. As if he were trying to sound tougher, dumber. Not the same kid who discussed the ozone layer or the Stockholm Syndrome. I guess he was busy selling "truth."

Still, I couldn't help but think about the Pegs and the Square. The image was an old cliché, square pegs in a round hole. But it was interesting how they picked it up and adapted it to themselves like some tribal cult.

I've always been a round peg in a round-holed world. Teachers like me, other kids want to elect me to student council or class president, coaches confide in me, I'm always the team captain (despite that performance problem I mentioned). I've never been able *not* to fit in, even if I wanted. Fitting in so perfectly makes you as invisible as if you didn't fit in at all. The problem was, even though to all appearances I fit in everywhere perfectly, I never *felt* as if I fit. The more people accepted and welcomed me, the more I felt like an impostor that they would soon discover was a fake. Eventually they would have to see that I, too, was a square peg. Then they'd come after me at night with pitchforks and torches, screaming my name, ramming down our front door with a fallen tree trunk, dragging me out of bed while thousands of plum-colored fingers tear at my flesh.

"You figure it out," Griffin said angrily. His brusque tone interrupted my daydreaming. "He's the county sheriff as well as the reverend of the only church within forty miles. You tell me if that's right. Why shouldn't he act like God? If you try to do what you want and he doesn't think it's 'right,' he trumps up some charge and tosses you in jail. Like with me. He doesn't give a shit!" Here Griffin went off on a tirade of obscenity that surprised me. His eyes blazed with anger, his face clenched into a scowl, he shook his fist like a tent-show preacher ranting against the devil.

I looked through the camera lens at him. It was amazing. Through the camera he looked like a trustworthy politician out to save the country. He was riveting to watch and to listen to and it occurred to me that there was no reason I could think of why he couldn't, if he wanted to, be the round peg in a round hole that I was. Through the camera, he looked like the perfect all-American boy indignant over the misuse of power, determined to fight injustice. He could just as easily be living my life.

Why wasn't he?

"Being locked up doesn't make you guilty any more than having the key makes you innocent. The only thing that it defines is whether you're the prisoner or the jailer. But guilt and innocence ought to be judged by what you do, not who you offend."

I watched Didra watching him. During his last few speeches she'd stopped consulting her notebook and had just stared at him while he spoke. Like she believed him. Worse, like she believed *in* him.

"That's an hour," I said, switching off the camera. "End of interview."

Didra swung around, but she must have seen something in my expression, because whatever she was going to say, she didn't. She just closed her notebook and said, "I've got enough."

I felt like a childish jerk, but I didn't like what I was seeing and I didn't feel like standing there doing nothing. My dad probably would have just kept taping—it wouldn't be logical to interfere, to throw a tantrum. But then, Dad lost Mom. Is that logical?

"Would you mind shooting the reverse angles, Eric?" Didra asked. Her voice wasn't angry, but it was a little cool.

"I'll do it," Griffin volunteered. "I could use the practice. Maybe some Hollywood type will see this, sign me up to act in a few movies, after which I'll take up directing." He walked over to the camera and peeked through it. "Yeah, this is cool. I could get used to this."

While Griffin shot the reverse angles, I went out to the car to get my bag. The car was just where I'd left it, mashed up against the pine tree. I examined the fender and tried to estimate how many hours pushing McDLTs and fries it would take to pay for it.

I unlocked the trunk and pulled my bag out. It was a small nylon sports bag with a change of underwear, some extra socks, a sweater, and toiletries in it. I unzipped the bag and looked inside. I couldn't remember exactly how I'd packed everything, so it was possible that Griffin had popped the trunk and rummaged through my bag, even though nothing was missing. Apparently he didn't break into things just to steal, sometimes just to break in. Like with my wallet or Didra's briefcase.

I looked over my shoulder. No one was looking. I went over to the passenger side and quietly opened the door. On the way out of D.C. I'd stopped at a drugstore and bought a box of condoms. They had a lot of different brands and different kinds. I tried to look like I was used to buying them, like I wasn't about to burst into flames from embarrassment. Finally I just grabbed whatever was in front of me, marched to the checkout stand, threw down the money, and left. I tossed the bag into the glove compartment and locked the door without ever looking in the bag, so I can't tell you what kind they were. I'd never actually used one before, but I was pretty sure I'd know how. I'd seen them sometimes on the streets or on the playgrounds at public schools. I could never figure out how they got there, what the circumstances might be that someone had to discard one next to the jungle gym.

I slid into the seat and stuck my key into the glove compartment lock. I turned the key, but the lock didn't budge. I tried again. Nothing. I pounded the compartment door. Nothing. I kicked the damn door. Nothing.

I got out of the car. The crash must have jammed the lock somehow. Did I need any more proof that I was being punished for some cosmic sin?

I walked back to the cabin, booting every stray stone or pine cone out of my way. When I walked into the cabin, Griffin was standing behind Didra, his arm wrapped around her throat, choking her to death.

15 ～

 $The\ first\ time$ I met Didra she was stepping out of her skirt.

"Oh," I'd said. "Sorry."

"Do you mind?" she'd said sternly.

"No, I don't," I'd said without thinking.

She'd laughed.

This was backstage during auditions for *A Midsummer Night's Dream.* I'd been looking for someplace quiet to rehearse my lines before my turn came up. Way in the back, behind the old painted scenery from last semester's production of *Our Town,* was a cubbyhole where they stored the costumes from the last ten years. It was a small and stuffy corner, usually abandoned. But when I came around the cardboard church, there was Didra, her plaid wraparound skirt in her hand. She wore black ribbed tights underneath and her shirttails hung down over her lap and behind like little aprons, so there was nothing to see. Even so, seeing her standing there folding her skirt made my throat dry up and my ears burn.

"Sorry," I said. "I didn't know you were back here."

She looked at me as if trying to decide whether or not I was a pervert. "You're Eric Marlowe, aren't you?"

"Yes."

She nodded, satisfied that I was okay. Like I said, I had a reputation for being a good guy. Even though she was a senior and I was a junior, and we had never met before, the movers and shakers of each class know who their counterparts are. She was editor of the school newspaper, I was class president; she was editor of the yearbook, I was captain of the basketball team; she was secretary of the French Club, I was treasurer of the German Club. Stuff like that.

Anyway, she knew I wasn't going to attack her or anything.

She rummaged through a rack of costumes. Her back was to me and I took the opportunity to stare at her legs. Even encased in black tights, I could see they were perfect. "So what part are you trying out for?" she asked, taking a costume off the rack.

"Oberon."

She turned and smiled. "Yeah, king of the faeries."

"It's a good part," I said defensively.

"It's the hardest part in the play."

"The most lines anyway."

She stepped into a short velour skirt she'd taken from the rack. The skirt had silver sequins in the shape of tiny stars. The Big Dipper and Orion glittered in front. "I'm trying out for Titania, your wife." She fastened the skirt and bunched up her white blouse above her waist. A tiny strip of pink skin showed between skirt top and shirt bottom. I stared at that pink strip of skin as if witnessing my first sunrise.

"What do you think?" she said. "Do I look like queen of the faeries?"

She looked like queen of the whole world.

"Looks nice," I said.

"I'm not that great of an actress, but Dr. Norton is such a horny teacher, I figured the more leg I show the better my chances."

Dr. Norton was over sixty, chairman of the English Department, and he directed all the plays. He was extremely bright, dedicated, a gifted director, and a conscientious teacher. But he did like to stare at the girls. I had the feeling that he wasn't staring at them out of sexual desire exactly, the look in his eyes seemed more like remembrance, as if he would look at a young girl and suddenly be transported back forty-five years to his own school days. Nobody minded much about his staring, because he never did anything about it. And when he caught himself he blushed so badly that students would giggle—not in front of him, of course, because no one wanted to hurt his feelings. He was probably the most liked teacher in the school. If a student, girl or boy, had any kind of personal or academic problem, he was the first one they went to. He just had that one little quirk.

"You look good," I said to Didra.

"The competition is tough this year." Didra looked down at herself and shook her head, not satisfied. She reached under her skirt and pulled her tights down to her ankles. Then she kicked off her shoes and stepped out of the tights altogether. She shook them out and folded them neatly over her plaid skirt. "Better?"

I wanted to say something, but I couldn't trust my voice from embarrassing me. I just nodded.

"I hope this doesn't take long. My legs are freezing." She strolled past me without looking back. I heard her voice echoing from the stage, " 'I'm ready for my close-up, Mr. DeMille.' ".

I heard Dr. Norton laugh. A couple of the kids laughed, too, probably not because they recognized the quote, but because Didra Lester had said it and so it must be funny. I knew the line came from an old movie, *Sunset Boulevard,* because Sunday nights are Dad's night to control the VCR. We have to watch whatever movies he rents. That one we must've seen three times already.

Didra and I both got the parts. Every day after school the entire cast rehearsed for two or three hours. We marched around the stage with our Washington Square paperback editions of the play, scribbling the blocking instructions as Dr. Norton directed us. Some of the kids had trouble remembering which was upstage and downstage until Dr. Norton yelled in frustration from the front row of the audience seats, "Toward me is downstage. Think of where I am as hell and if you move toward me, you're going *down* toward hell. Downstage!"

That seemed to work.

Didra and I didn't have many scenes together, and the ones we did have were mostly fighting. We were supposed to be married, but we argued a lot. Later in the play we got to kiss and make up, but it seemed to be taking weeks for us to get to that part. Except for the donkey head that one of the other characters wore, none of us had costumes yet, so I never got another chance to see Didra changing clothes.

"Now kiss," Dr. Norton said one day.

We kissed. On stage. In front of the whole cast. As I lowered my head toward hers, I could hear Brenda Tilly giggling in the wings. She was in charge of costumes. Vinnie Gianerro, who did the lighting and was in my calculus class, stood next to Brenda and made loud sucking noises against his forearm. "Go for it, Eric," he hooted.

I don't know how long the kiss lasted, maybe a second, it was nothing more than me brushing my lips against hers and pulling away, like a bee sniffing a flower without landing. But in that fraction of a second when our lips touched, all my senses kicked into turbocharge. I smelled her shampoo and soap, tasted her lip gloss (not lipstick, just something to protect her lips from the bitter cold outside—it was December). She must have let out a little breath as I touched her, because I felt the warmth against my chin. My whole body shivered as if a fingernail had suddenly been dragged up my spine. I wondered if forty-five years from now I'd be staring at young girls and remembering this moment.

I know it sounds like I'm making a big deal out of a little kiss, but that's how it felt. I'd kissed before, lots of long passionate evenings with my face clamped against Ann Marie Thompson's or Brooke Glick's, hands sliding up and down their bodies, buttons and zippers being fumbled open. But this was different. Special.

I couldn't tell if Didra felt the same way. If she did, she was very good at hiding it. She just delivered her lines and walked off.

That night I started writing my own play about two people in summer stock somewhere in Vermont. I'd never been to Vermont, but it seemed to be the kind of romantic place where anything could happen. Anyway, this man and woman are in a play in which their characters are supposed to be lovers. But each of the actors in real life has a boyfriend or girlfriend, who's also acting in the play. I called the guy Paris and the woman Helen, because I thought you had to have some allusions to Greek mythology for it to be a real play. As the play progresses, our Paris and Helen fall deeper and deeper in love. Only they never talk about how they feel toward each other, they just speak their lines in the play within the play. But as their love grows, they try to communicate their love in the way they deliver their lines. By the end of the play, they are so good in their roles that they are discovered and offered big parts in films and Broadway. They leave Vermont with their original boyfriend and girlfriend, never having said to each other how they really felt, except through the words of the play they were in.

Too romantic, you think?

When we weren't actually onstage, most of my time backstage was spent memorizing lines, finding someone to cue me while I tried to recite all that blank verse that Shakespeare wrote. I don't think if he'd had to memorize it himself he'd have been so clever in all those speeches. Usually I ran my lines with Phil Butler, who played Nick Bottom. Sometimes the memorizing got to both of us and we'd borrow a couple of swords from the prop boxes and have a great sword fight in the hallway next to the cafeteria. The way the clanging swords echoed made it sound like a movie. Sometimes we got carried away and whacked each other pretty hard. I laid a welt on his arm that didn't go away until the end of the play. I still have a small scar on my knuckles where he jabbed me.

It would have been natural for Didra and me to rehearse our scenes together, but she was dating Lenny Fowler, the football quarterback, National Honor Society Member, and the president of the senior class. I knew him from some of the school functions and a few parties, enough to chat with about how our teams were doing. He was a nice guy, but I'd heard he had a jealous streak and had shoved Dennis Lamar to the ground in the parking lot when he gave Didra a ride to school. So rehearsing with Didra could prove hazardous to my health.

"You want to run some lines?" she asked me one day at rehearsal.

"Sure," I said without hesitation.

She'd already memorized all her lines, so I was the one who needed the most prompting. I think I was blowing more lines than usual because I was anticipating the scene where we kiss and I didn't know what she'd expect me to do. If I kissed her, she might think I was coming on to her. If I didn't, she might think I was a wimp. The whole time I kept picking at the Band-Aid on my knuckle where Phil had gouged me with his sword.

When we got to the kissing part I said, "And then we kiss. Kiss, kiss."

Didra laughed. "Is that what you tell your girlfriend on a date? 'Kiss, kiss.' "

"Yup. Saves wear and tear on the lips. I figure every pair of lips only has so many kisses in it, like a tank of gas can only go so many miles. So I'd better conserve for the right person."

"With all that conserving, how are you going to know the right person?"

"I guess you're just supposed to know. Like Cary Grant and Ingrid Bergman."

"*Indiscreet.*"

"Yes." I smiled. That was another of Dad's Sunday night favorites. But I ended up liking it a lot.

Didra looked at me a long time. Then she leaned forward and kissed me. I knew right away this was no stage kiss. This was the real thing.

Now, at the time, I was sort of dating Melanie Landers, who always made the sign of the cross whenever we drove past St. Ann's church. She was *very* Catholic. Despite that, she enjoyed some torrid petting and she was a pretty good athlete, the star of the girls' soccer team. But I knew the moment I finished kissing Didra I would have to break it off with Melanie. Even if I hadn't started dating Didra, there was no way I could go back to Melanie's lips. They were nice lips and all, but they just weren't Didra's.

As it turned out, Didra and I did a lot of kissing after that. I don't know what she told Lenny Fowler, but he seemed to take it fairly well, though that pretty much ended our little chats about how the teams were doing. You'd think in this day and age it wouldn't be a big deal anymore when a senior girl dates a junior boy, but it is. She wasn't even a whole year older, just nine months, but everyone acted like she was robbing the cradle. Some of the hostility came from senior boys who'd been hitting on Didra for years without success. Of course, I was a hero in the junior class, the kid who'd bagged Didra Lester. Girls in my classes flirted with me more than ever and I had to admit I kind of liked the notoriety.

We'd been going together for about two months when I first showed her my play about the summer stock in Vermont. Our school play had been over for a week and everyone agreed it had been a big success. There was an awkward moment on Friday night when I forgot a couple of lines in a long speech, but nobody noticed except Dr. Norton and Dad.

We were in my bedroom when I gave her my play. It was called *Off Stage*. I could hear Steely Dan drifting down the hall from Dad's study, where he was grading papers. He didn't mind that Didra was in my room, or that the door was closed. We'd already had the father-son talk about sex three years ago, so I knew all about responsibility and that I was free to do it whenever I thought it was right. He had first had sex when he was fifteen and Mom when she was sixteen. Didra had never been specific, but I got the distinct impression that she and Lenny Fowler had done it for over a year now. I was seventeen and still hadn't, which put a strange kind of pressure on me.

Didra stretched out on my bed and kept reading, turning page after page, laughing sometimes, looking intense other times. I sat at my desk and pretended to study, though I kept looking up to watch her reflection in my fish tank. She was wearing her plaid skirt and one leg was bent so I could see up her dress if I wanted. But I was more interested in her face, in her reaction to my play. I wondered if that was an unhealthy sign. Maybe that was the reason Mom and Dad had both beat me to the punch, sexually speaking.

When she finished, she straightened the pages into a neat pile and stretched her arms and legs. I could see her in the fish tank, but I didn't turn around. I kept on pretending to study.

"You're such a jerk," she said, laughing.

"What?"   ·

"What? You. You're such a jerk. You're dying to ask me what I think. So go ahead."

I turned around. "Okay, what do you think?"

"I'm not telling you until you come over here." She patted the bed next to her. "Come on."

I got up and laid down next to her, my hand on her stomach. "Speak, woman. But remember how sensitive I am." I batted my lashes real fast and she laughed.

"I loved it, Eric. I really did."

My stomach kind of hiccuped, a spasm of relief. I didn't know what I'd have done if she hadn't liked it. How would I have been able to go out with her after such humiliation?

"It's not finished yet," I said. "It still needs a couple of scenes, some polishing here and there—"

"I like it just the way it is. It's sad, but there are a lot of funny lines in it. It's like I saw a whole side of you I didn't know was there. I'm impressed." She kissed me, pulling me on top of her. "Now I know you're worthy of me." She laughed and kissed me again. This went on for quite a while. Steely Dan became Cat Stevens.

"Maybe we should both try out for the next school play, in the spring," I said. I thought she'd be excited at the prospect.

"Not me," she said. "Once is enough."

"I thought you liked it."

"Some of it. I liked getting to know you." She kissed me again. "But I just did it to be able to put it on my application. The good colleges want their students well-rounded." She hopped off the bed and leaned over next to my aquarium. She made a fish face, opening and closing her pursed lips like a fish. "What do you think?"

"Uncanny."

"Yeah, not bad."

"Maybe you can put 'does fish impressions' on your application."

She straightened up and gave me a serious look. "You mad about something?"

"No."

"You're acting like it."

"I'm not mad." But I was, a little. I don't know why, something to do with her reason for acting in the play. But that was stupid of me. What difference did that make now? I gestured for her to return to the bed. She did. We kissed until Cat Stevens became Bob Dylan.

16

Less than a second passed, but in that fevered second I saw everything sharply focused, like a sniper tracking his victim through a rifle scope.

I saw Griffin's thick forearm clamped against Didra's throat. The reptilian tail of his tattoo poked out from under his sleeve, the blue scales rubbing obscenely against Didra's hostage jaw. Both her small hands tugged at his arm, but without much energy, as if she were on the verge of blacking out. Suddenly Griffin arched his back and lifted Didra off her feet. She dangled from his arm as if she were hanged.

I don't remember ever moving that fast before, not ever. Without thinking I bounded across the room, hurdled the sofa, and dove for him with a wrestling tackle I hadn't used since junior varsity.

"Eric!" Didra yelled as the three of us toppled to the floor.

The impact must have weakened his grip on her, because

she rolled free of him and kept rolling until she smacked into the driftwood table in front of the sofa. Even as I was wrestling with Griffin I heard her head thud against the wood.

"Jesus, Eric!" Griffin said. He was grabbing for my wrists the way Didra had earlier.

I twisted free. The wrestling coach would have been proud of my dexterity, my fierceness. Takedown and escape, I was way ahead in points. I moved now as I never had while on the team—with purpose. But I didn't think about that then. I just started grabbing twisting body parts. But he was stronger than I'd expected, shaking my holds off. Finally, in frustrated rage, I abandoned the ritualized sport of wrestling and started flailing at him with my fists, swinging wildly at his face. I know I connected a few times, because I felt a knuckle on my left hand pop.

"Eric, for God's sake!"

Didra's voice. But distant, like a fog horn.

More immediate was Griffin. I was straddling him, still punching away. But he had reached up with one hand and palmed my face as if it were a basketball about to be slam-dunked. Two of his fingers were digging into my eyes while his thumb was hooked under my chin, crushing my windpipe. I'd never experienced this kind of dirty fighting before, so it threw me for a moment. I grabbed his hand and tried to apply a wristlock, but he used his other hand to stab into my kidneys. It wasn't a punch, it was a stiff, flat hand like a shovel. What the hell kind of fight was this? My eyes watered from the pain, but I kept punching blindly.

"Stop it, Eric!" Didra said. Closer now. Her warm breath against my cheek. Her hands clutching my arms, pulling me off Griffin.

Which is when Griffin punched me.

It was a looping roundhouse, clubbing me directly in the

left temple. I was surprised at the power of his punch. And at the thundering pain. At first I thought my skull had collapsed from the impact, but I felt the area with my fingertips. No visible damage. Except that my whole head felt as if a dentist were drilling into my brain. Little pinpoints of light flared and popped in front of my eyes. I sagged into Didra's arms.

"You didn't have to hit him!" she yelled.

"He was hitting me!" Griffin yelled back.

"I was holding his arms!"

"That's the best time to hit someone!"

Their argument didn't need me. Anyway, I was more interested in the sputter of sparks swirling dizzily before me.

Griffin climbed slowly to his feet. I blinked rapidly, but I couldn't get the haze to go away. It was like looking through a dirty screen door. Blood was dripping from his stitched wound. But he didn't wipe the blood. He didn't take his eyes off me. He was in his caveman crouch, the hunched attack position he'd gone into two hours ago when the sheriff had first knocked on the door. He looked as if he wanted to finish me off by sinking his teeth into my throat.

I noticed I was kneeling and tried to climb to my feet also. A sudden cramp in my kidney shoved me back to my knees. I took a deep breath.

"Take your time, Eric," Didra said, her hand on my shoulder.

"He . . . choking . . . you," I rasped.

"No, sweetheart, no. He was just demonstrating how he put that guy in the hospital. That guy the sheriff told us about. It was self-defense really. He had no choice."

I tried again to stand. The pain kicked my side again, but I fought it. The screen door was gone, but there was still some lint around the edges.

"Hey, sorry, man," Griffin said. "I was just protecting myself. You flew at me like a madman." He offered his hand to shake.

What should I do? The fight really was my fault. I jumped to conclusions and threw the first punch. But I needed more time to think this whole thing through, analyze everything, assign responsibility, determine an appropriate course of action. Yet there was his hand, floating in front of me. He smiled expectantly. Didra watched me. I had to do something.

I shook his hand without enthusiasm.

"Quite a wallop you pack, dude," he said, rubbing his jaw.

I looked down at my left hand. One of the knuckles was swollen to the size of a golf ball. It hurt some, but I wasn't going to show any more pain to him.

Didra picked up the fireplace brush and shovel, which we'd knocked over in our fighting. I hadn't even noticed. "Griffin said the guy attacked him in the shower."

"In the shower?" I said skeptically. "I think I've seen that movie."

"Where do you think the movies get those stories?"

"From other movies," I said.

"Yeah, well, somewhere down the line they got it from someone who knows. Someone who's stood naked in the shower and had some kid the size of an ox with a brain rivaled in intelligence only by mashed potatoes. Then this ox-size kid is pissed at you because you said something about him, or he thinks you said something about him, or he doesn't like your tattoo, or he likes the way you look naked." He looked at Didra. She looked away and straightened a pillow. There was a small purple knob on her forehead where she'd bumped into the driftwood table.

"Which was it for you?" I asked. "Why did he come after you?"

"Take your pick. Maybe all of the above. With some of these guys, who knows? They aren't logical beings." He smiled at me. "Not like you and me, bro."

I pointed to his forehead. "You've popped some stitches. You're bleeding."

He shrugged. "It'll keep."

"So what happened?" Didra asked.

"So this ox pulls a knife. Not no homemade blade, no prison shiv. Son of a bitch has some kinda goddamn bowie knife or something. Comes at me like he's gonna butcher a hog." Griffin picked up some fallen magazines and placed them on the driftwood table. *Connoisseur, National Geographic, Life, Yachting.* His eyes lingered on them a moment, his fingers stroking the glossy cover of *Yachting.* "Anyway, I got him in that hold I was showing you, Didra. Only I didn't hold back none. I cinched my arm against his throat so tight I thought my tattoo was gonna rub off on his jaw."

"You wouldn't have killed him?" Didra asked.

Griffin smiled at her. "Guess we'll never know. A guard clubbed me unconscious before we found out. Later the guard claimed I slipped on the soap."

"That's not fair!" Didra said, outraged.

I expected Griffin to say something clever, something about how the world wasn't fair to anyone Behind Locked Doors. Something to put himself in the light of the romantic outlaw that he liked to bask in for Didra. But all he said, and this he mumbled more to himself than us, was, "Who's to say what's fair?"

I went out to the kitchen and returned with some ice cubes in a plastic bag. The cubes hadn't had enough time to

freeze completely since dinner, so mostly it was chipped ice.
I pressed it against Didra's forehead.

"Ouch." She pushed the ice away.

"You've got a bump. This will help."

"A bump?" She touched her forehead, winced. She hurried down the hall to the bathroom. "Oh, *damn!*"

When she came back, she was walking slowly. She opened her hand and I gave her the ice bag. She clamped it to her forehead and sat on the sofa. "At least we did the videotape before this."

Griffin went over to the video camera and ejected the tape. "What are you going to do with this?"

"I don't know yet. My father has a few connections at D.C. news stations. I might be able to get this on the air."

"Just don't let them edit too much. They can change the whole meaning. Cut the heart out."

"I don't think I'll have too much control over that."

He turned and glared at her. "Try."

"Let's turn in," I said to Didra. I held out my hand. When she took it I pulled her to her feet and led her down the hall.

"There's linen and blankets in that closet," she called over her shoulder. "The sofa folds out into a bed."

"I'll figure it out," Griffin said. "You two have a nice night now. Don't worry about me, I'm a heavy sleeper. Nothing wakes me up, no amount of noise."

When we were in the bedroom I closed the door behind me and leaned against it with a sigh. "Finally."

"I missed you, too, sweetheart," Didra said. She thought my "finally" referred to our being alone. Actually, I'd meant that I was finally away from Griffin. I didn't tell her that.

She dropped the ice bag on the dresser and stepped into my arms. We kissed. The kiss was going pretty well, too, until my forehead bumped her bruise and she cried out in pain into my mouth.

"I'm sorry," I said.

"Me too. I know this isn't the romantic evening either of us planned."

I smiled and pulled her close. "The evening's not over."

17 〜

This part gets a little embarrassing, but I guess you have to know about it to understand what happened later.

First of all, I never expected that the first time Didra and I would be alone together with the express purpose of making love, an escaped convict would be sleeping in the next room. No matter how much I tried to ignore Griffin, I kept picturing him right outside the door, his ear suctioned to the wood, his fist pressed into his mouth to keep from laughing.

"How's the head?" I asked as I unbuttoned my shirt. I was trying to sound casual, cavalier, as if getting undressed together was something we did nightly. But my thumbs and fingers suddenly felt as swollen as knackwursts and each little shirt button seemed greased with Crisco.

"Fine," she said.

We were standing on opposite sides of her parents' brass bed with our backs turned to each other. The room was dark except for the moonlight that filtered through the filigree curtains.

Didra was unbuttoning her blouse and I could see her reflection in the dresser mirror. She was wearing a cream-colored slip.

It was kind of funny standing back to back like we were about to start pacing off for a duel. We had each touched each other pretty much everywhere there is to touch before, and we'd seen all the various parts of each other's anatomy before. But never the whole body. It's not like any of the parts had changed since the last time we saw each other, it was just kind of intimidating because we both knew there'd be a moment where we looked at each other's bodies and made a judgment. I felt pretty confident because I'd been lifting weights and running a lot more since we'd decided on this weekend three months ago.

Now that we were about to consummate our relationship, I didn't know why I'd waited so long. It really wasn't a sense of morality, I don't think. There'd been times during the past couple of years when I was so fevered with lust that I was afraid they'd have to lock me up to keep women on the streets safe. But then there were times with some girls when I'd had the opportunity—they'd been eager—but I'd backed off. Not because I was afraid, not because I didn't want to, but because I knew I didn't care enough for them. Not that they all were in love with me. Some, I think, didn't care who they were with. When I turned them down, they found someone else five minutes later to disappear with. And it's not that I'm some crazy romantic who feels you have to be in love, that there has to be music and flowers and vows. I guess that's the problem—I don't know what I feel. All I know is that it seemed important to me that when I was done making love, I'd want to hold the girl in my arms and smell her hair and be as happy just lying there with her as I was while we were making love.

I glanced into the mirror. Didra's skirt and blouse were off. She stood in her slip and pantyhose, folding her skirt neatly the way she had that first day we'd met. Although the room was dark, her blond hair was the kind that reflected even the tiniest bit of light in a dark room. She was slim, athletic-looking, even a little boyish. I mean, she didn't have much in the way of breasts. But there was something in the way she held herself, completely fearless, as if she had total confidence in whatever she did. She lifted her slip above her hips and began to peel off her pantyhose. I felt a jab in my heart almost as powerful as the one Griffin had given me earlier in my kidney. God, she was gorgeous. But right then, in her slip and the dim light, she looked a little like a ghost.

I looked away from the mirror. If she'd wanted me to watch her undress, she wouldn't be facing away from me. And if she didn't want me to watch, I should at least give her that much privacy.

I had my shirt unbuttoned, but I didn't take it off. I sat on the edge of the bed and took off my shoes and socks. I wasn't sure what to do next.

Didra's briefcase was laying next to me on the bed. I thought of Griffin's stubby fingers picking through it and I got angry at him. I wanted to go out and start pounding on his face again. I looked at my swollen knuckle and heard the rustle of nylon behind me and decided fighting could wait.

I was stalling I guess, but I reached over and took Didra's notebook out of the briefcase. It was one of those blue three-ring binders, the same kind she carried in high school. She used to draw my initials in the cover, big and elaborate like medieval letters from a wizard's book of spells. This notebook didn't have anything drawn on the cover. I opened it and smiled. She'd filled in the class schedule on the preprinted grid that comes on the inside of the cover. Just like high school. She was the only person I knew who actually did that.

"Got any of your articles in here for me to read?" I asked.

I felt her weight on the bed behind me, the rustle of the bedcovers. I looked over my shoulder. She was under the covers, the blanket up to her neck. Her slip and pantyhose were folded on top of her skirt on the rocking chair. She didn't wear a bra.

"You sure reading's what you want to do now?" She smiled.

"Good point." I stood up to finish undressing. First I reached over to close her notebook, when I noticed the names of her courses inked neatly into the little boxes of the schedule. "What's this you're taking? Broadcast Journalism. Introduction to Acting. Photography 122. What's Photography 122?"

She sighed. "Videotaping."

I looked at her. "Where are the journalism courses?"

"Broadcast Journalism, right there. Mondays and Fridays, noon till two."

"That's not journalism, Didra. That's TV."

"Thank you, Dan Rather."

"You know what I mean."

"What are you, my parent or my boyfriend?"

"That's crap, Didra. You hate TV news. You and I used to watch it and laugh at the stories all the time. The way they interview actors during the news who just happen to have a series on that same channel. That stupid way the anchors ask each other questions that they've already rehearsed. The goddamn news stories about some little girl trapped somewhere that they keep milking day after day, with choked-up expressions. That's not journalism, that's show business."

"Not all of it. Some, sure, but it doesn't have to be. TV can do just as good a job as newspapers. Better sometimes."

"No, it can't. Not as long as every broadcast is measured by the ratings and not by the quality. That's something you told me yourself."

Didra didn't say anything. She was looking at the patchwork quilt covering her, a handmade thing that probably took some woman in the Appalachian Mountains a month to make, for which she got a hundred of the thousand dollars it must have cost. Didra wrung the edge of the quilt in her hands.

I know I was being stupid. This wasn't the time to argue. But what the hell, nothing else had gone right today. And I was angry that she hadn't told me, that she'd had another secret to go along with smoking. "Remember what we used to talk about? You were going to write the facts and I was going to write the truth. Your articles, my plays. That's what we planned."

"Christ, Eric, grow up. That was high school. This is college. It's a whole new world. Facts and truth, Eric? Give me a break."

I guess it did sound silly now. But why hadn't it when we'd sat in the park under the sun, holding hands and saying exactly the same thing?

There were tears in Didra's eyes, which scared me a little, because I'd never seen her cry before. "You always want to see the stories I write. You want to know why I never showed them to you, why I always had an excuse? Well, I don't write any stories, that's why. I'm a lousy writer."

"No, you're not. You were editor of the school paper."

"Big goddamn deal. I didn't have to write anything. All I

had to do was tell someone else what to write. That's all I did."

"What about the editorials?"

"Joyce Blair wrote them. I told her what slant to take and she wrote them for me."

I was stunned. Many times we had discussed her editorials before she wrote them, debating her position.

"So what," I said softly. "That's why they have writing courses at college. You can learn."

"Jesus." She shook her head in the dark. "You don't understand. I tried that. I started the semester in a newspaper writing course. I was the worst in the class. That's why I switched to broadcast journalism. I may look stupid in print, but for some reason I look good on camera."

I climbed onto the bed, still in my pants, and sat next to her, holding both her hands in one of mine. "You can do anything you set your mind to, Didra. You're the most determined girl I know."

"Sure, in high school. That's what I'm telling you. Everything I've done has been through hard work. Nothing comes easy. I read, I study, I memorize. I write thorough but bland essays. That's how I got good grades. But writing articles isn't just memorizing, it's something you do well or you don't. You do it well, I don't."

I thought of all the stories and poems and scenes I'd written that were so awful I buried them in boxes up in the rafters of the garage. "It's just a skill," I said. "Something you learn. Like tennis."

"Why bother? I'm already good at broadcasting. Besides, Daddy says that's where the future is. I've done some sample videotapes and Daddy thinks he can get me a summer internship at WBTM. Not on-camera reporting or anything, but something at the station. It'll look great on my résumé."

"WBTM? Where's that?"

"Baltimore."

"Baltimore? Didra, we have plans, remember? Spend the summer together here while I finish summer school, then I transfer to college with you."

"I'm sorry, Eric. Daddy pulled a lot of strings to get me this job. It's a great opportunity."

"Your father could have gotten you a job in D.C."

She shrugged. She knew it was true.

I thought about Mr. Lester, smiling at me last summer. Treating me like his best buddy, the son he never had. And Mrs. Lester in her cream-colored outfit, blond and regal. Smiling as if she were already making our wedding plans. They must have decided right then that they'd find some way to keep Didra away from me. And all this time I'd been convinced they liked me. How could I have misjudged them so badly?

"Jesus, Didra," I snapped. "Jesus!"

"Baltimore is not that far away, Eric," Didra said.

"Yes, it is. Just not in miles."

We looked at each other. In the dark her eyes were flat and colorless, like those button eyes on dolls.

"Why'd you come here this weekend without telling me all this first?"

"I didn't think it mattered that much. That you'd make such a big deal about it."

"You didn't think it mattered? That we weren't going to spend the summer together? We had *plans,* for God's sake. Plans for our future together. What else haven't you told me? That you've been sleeping with someone else?"

I didn't say it because I thought it was true. I said it because it was so outlandish that it would make my point.

However, when I saw the way her eyes flicked away from mine, I knew right then it was true.

My stomach sort of seized up and I couldn't catch my breath. The old basketball game choke-in-the-clutch attack. I was panting through my mouth but trying to be quiet about it so she wouldn't know how much it hurt. I wondered if Dad had the same reaction when he heard about Mom and Dr. Askers. Did his eyes burn as if someone had splashed acid in them? Did his skin shrink suddenly until it was too tight? Did his insides start to clench and unclench as if they were strangling each other?

I looked at her blond hair glowing in the dark like those plastic figurines for dashboards. I tried to make out the features of her face, but the shadows were too dark. It occurred to me that right at that moment, I couldn't really remember what she looked like in the light.

18 ～

"Hand me my purse," Didra said.

I climbed off the bed. I walked on legs that didn't feel like mine. These legs didn't fit properly. They were too long or too short or maybe they were on backward, because every step was awkward, as if I might suddenly pitch forward onto the floor.

"On the rocker," she pointed.

I went to the rocking chair. Her purse was under her pile of clothes. I handed it to her.

She rummaged through it, digging all the way to the bottom. She came up with a new pack of Salems and a disposable lighter. She unwrapped the pack, plucked out a cigarette, and lit it. She sighed and smoke blasted from her mouth. "God, I needed that."

I moved her clothes to the dresser and sat in the rocker. I rocked a little, each movement causing a harsh squeak either in the rocker or the wooden floorboards. I couldn't tell which.

"Now what?" she asked.

"What do you mean?"

"I mean, now what do we do? Are you going to ignore me, give me the silent treatment?"

"No," I said. "I just don't know what to say."

"What are you thinking?"

I was thinking that I wasn't a very good judge of character. That I had thought Mr. and Mrs. Lester were great folks who really liked me. That Didra was a dedicated writer anxious for a career in newspapers. That she loved me and wouldn't even think about sleeping with anyone else.

"What are you feeling?" she asked.

"Is this an interview? Don't you want the video camera running?"

She didn't say anything for a long time. Neither did I. She smoked. I rocked.

"Things are different at college," Didra finally said.

"You keep saying that. I go to the university, too, you know."

"That's not the same. That's one class. And you still live at home. It's different when you're all on your own. There's so much going on. So many choices. And when you blow it, there's no one to turn to."

"There's me."

She shook her head while she exhaled and smoke wagged back and forth around her face. In the dim light the smoke looked like strands of wispy blond hair added to her own. She looked different now, unfamiliar.

"I wanted to talk to you about it. But Daddy said he could help."

"And he did. Helped push us apart." I rocked and listened to the squeaks. "Who's the guy?"

"What difference does it make?"

I rocked some more. "None."

"Just a guy. He's in my Broadcast Journalism class. His father is Jordan March, the anchor on WWDC."

I nodded. Of the D.C. newscasts, WWDC was the best. Jordan March seemed pretty no-nonsense about his job too. Didra and I had agreed that he was probably the least offensive of the local bunch. Which didn't make me feel any better.

There was another long silence, punctuated by the steady squeaking of my chair as I rocked slowly back and forth. I liked the movement and figured I could probably keep this up all night. Maybe for days.

"Come to bed, Eric," she said after a while. "Just come to bed, okay?"

I didn't say anything, I was too into my rocking.

"We don't have to do anything. We can just sleep."

"When were you going to tell me about him? Or were you?"

She shrugged, tugged the quilt tight to her neck. "I don't know. I love you, you know that. But my life isn't going as I thought it would. Nothing is."

"We had plans."

"Plans change. This weekend's events should prove that much." Her voice caught as if she were going to cry, but she wouldn't let herself. "I don't know what to tell you. I didn't want these things to happen. They just did."

"Which leaves us where?"

She took a puff of her cigarette. The tip glowed neon-red in the dark. "I don't know. Without plans, I guess. We'll have to see."

"And if I crawled into bed with you right now, you'd make love to me?"

"Yes."

"But when you go back to school you'll probably do the same thing with this March kid?"

"Yes."

"Does he know about me?"

"Yes."

"Does he mind?"

"Yes."

Each of her *yeses* punctured my chest like steel darts. I didn't know what to say. I couldn't find the logic in what she was doing, I couldn't understand the reason in what she was feeling. My questions and her answers made me feel as if I were a detective giving a lie detector test about some heinous crime. Except I was the one bleeding.

I heard a noise and I fired a glance over my shoulder. It sounded like another floorboard squeak, only this one coming from the hallway just outside the door. "Did you hear that?"

"What?" Didra said.

"Nothing." What difference did it make if Griffin was skulking outside the door? If he heard, so what? I looked at Didra. "So now what? Do we break up or what?"

"I don't know. Is that what you want?"

"Are you going to keep sleeping with that other guy?"

She stubbed out her cigarette. "Probably. I'm not planning it or anything. I don't have much faith in plans anymore."

"But if it happens, it happens. Right?"

"I guess so."

"I don't know how you can live that way."

"I know you don't. I don't know either. I just am." She smiled sadly. "It's not so bad."

I rocked slowly. How can she live without plans and a schedule and a program on how to achieve those plans. I know exactly what I'm going to do for the next five years and I have a tentative schedule for the five years after that. I don't mean every day or anything stupid like that. Just kind of where I want to go and how I'm going to get there. Like setting out for a trip through some backwoods state you've never been. I mean, you'd take a map, wouldn't you? That's all I'm saying. I had a mental map of my future. My dad teases me about it, says I have more five-year plans than China. He thinks I plan too much. I don't tell him, but I think that maybe if he'd planned more, Mom wouldn't have left us.

"Come to bed, Eric," she said softly.

I got up from my rocker, stripped off my clothes except for my underpants, and climbed into bed. She curved her back into my chest. I wrapped my arms around her. I felt the warmth of her skin from her neck to the balls of her feet. Her hair pressed against my nose and I could smell the smoke and steak and shampoo.

"Good night," I said, and closed my eyes.

There was a silence, as if she were waiting for something more. After a while, she said good night too.

19 ≋

Here's what happened on that awful trip to Hawaii: The morning I landed in Hawaii there were no native girls waiting to throw flowered leis around my neck. No one shoved a drink garnished with tropical fruit in my hand. No one said "Aloha." Not like in the movies.

Of course, this was just the small island of Kauai and the airport looked more like a rundown bus station. It was Easter week, but nobody getting off the plane looked all that happy to be here. That could've had something to do with the flight from Honolulu to here, which got a little bumpy over the ocean. One girl my age barfed the whole way here. You could see people turning away from her, their faces scrunched and sick-looking as she continued to make those awful grunting noises. People covered their noses with handkerchiefs, sleeves, magazines, anything to filter the smell. I felt sorry for her, but I have to admit, I turned away and smothered my nose too. My stomach had gotten queasy just hearing her. The stewardess changed the girl's air-sickness bag twice, and just when you thought the poor kid was done and on the verge of passing out, you'd hear another gurgle that got louder and louder and then she'd grab her gut and double over and start spewing again. I looked for her in the airport, because I hadn't really seen her face on the plane, just the back of her head. I was curious whether she was pretty or not, because I had trouble imagining a pretty girl barfing.

"Chipmunk!" my mom hollered.

I turned and saw her running through the crowded terminal toward me, her arms open, making happy cooing noises as she approached. My mom's not afraid of expressing herself in public, no matter where she is or who's watching. Nothing embarrasses her. However, I hate having people stare at me, so I avoid public displays of affection.

"Chipmunk!" she screamed again, though I was right in front of her now. She threw her arms around me and hugged tight. I have to admit, I did the same. It felt pretty good.

The first thing I noticed was that her smell had changed. My nose was next to her neck and the usual mixture of Tuxedo perfume and oil paints was gone. She smelled earthier somehow, like sweet mud by a river bank.

She stood away from me and held me at arm's length, looking me over. She had the biggest smile on her face. Tears hung on the edges of her eyelashes. A couple of blinks and they would launch down her face like torpedoes.

"Jesus, Chip. Jesus!" She shook me, hugged me again.

Okay, you might as well know why she calls me Chipmunk. Mom likes to give animal nicknames to people she cares about. A little legacy from her ban-the-bomb, yin-and-yang, back-to-nature days. She selected Chipmunk for me because as a kid I was obsessed with Alvin and the Chipmunks. Every day, I played their records over and over, then my friends and I would walk around the house talking like them. We even did it in school until my fifth-grade teacher, Mrs. Grendal, sent a nasty note home to our parents. Sometimes I still talk like Alvin, just to tease Mom. Now she gets a kick out of it. Mom's nickname for Dad was Tad. After a tadpole. About ten years ago, Dad decided he needed to get in better shape, so he took up swimming laps at the university pool. He was an awful swimmer, with jerky spastic strokes and no rhythm to his kicks. He flopped around like a drowning man. But that didn't stop him. Once he'd made up his mind, he went every day and swam a hundred laps. They were a hundred ugly laps, but he did it. So Mom called him Tadpole. Corny, but it was better than what she'd called him before that: Doodles! Don't ask.

"God, look at you," Mom said. She held my face in her hands and stared at me. "Just look at you."

"I'm a knockout, aren't I?"

She laughed. "You're still a smart ass." Oh yeah, Mom wasn't one for watching her language. She pretty much said whatever came into her mind.

"I missed you, Mom," I said.

"You better have."

"No, I mean it. I really missed you."

She looked at my eyes and the smile wilted on her face. She sighed and hugged me close again. She whispered, "I missed you, too, honey. God, I miss you."

"Where's Dr. Askers?"

She pushed away from me, her smile back in place. But the tears had escaped and her cheeks were streaked. "He's back at the house. He figured we'd want this time alone."

I hated it that he was being so understanding.

"And don't go around calling him Dr. Askers. His name

is Tom and he's been asking you to call him that for a year now."

"I'm showing respect for my elders."

"You're being a jerk."

I laughed. She didn't say it mean or angry, just matter-of-fact, like, "You've got spinach stuck in your teeth." I'd forgotten how that could make me laugh.

We went to pick up my luggage, but it never came. After about thirty minutes of staring at revolving suitcases and backpacks and duffel bags, we reported my missing suitcase to the airline clerk. She didn't seem surprised. She said they'd call as soon as they found it.

Mom tossed me the keys to her Jeep. "Drive, hotshot."

As much as I fought it, I couldn't help but be impressed by the countryside. The sugarcane fields, the mountains crowned with clouds, the lushness of everything. The trees and plants were all so huge they made me feel smaller. But the neat part was that they made all my problems or worries seem smaller, too, as if the landscape were saying, "How, in the presence of all this magnificence, can your troubles be that bad?"

"How's your father?" Mom asked as I drove.

"Fine. You know."

"You taking care of him?"

"He doesn't need much watering, Mom."

She laughed. "Smart-ass punk. I raised a smart-ass punk."

Mom's house was more of a cottage really. I'm not sure what the original color of the paint was, but what little paint hadn't peeled or chipped off resembled moldy green. Next to the house was a huge garage made of corrugated steel. The garage was bigger than the house, big enough to park four cars side by side.

Dr. Askers stood just outside the garage using a canoe paddle to stir something thick in a large trash can. He was wearing bib overalls with no shirt underneath. His arms and back were tan and matted with thick black hair. A plump belly pushed out at his overalls. Not slim and muscled like Dad.

"Hey." He waved. "You found your way back home."

I hated that he called this place home. Our home was five thousand miles away from this dump.

Mom waved to him. "C'mere and check out my little heartthrob."

Dr. Askers scraped the canoe paddle on the edge of the rubber trash can. The stuff he was stirring looked like some kind of white paste. He wiped his hands on the thighs of his overalls. He stuck his hand out toward me as he approached. White crud still stuck to his fingers.

"Hey, kiddo," he said. "Long time no see."

"Hi, Tom," I said, shaking his hand.

Mom smiled and patted my shoulder. "I know you can't have grown any, but you look bigger."

"An illusion caused by my startling good looks," I said.

"Well, I've gotten bigger," Dr. Askers said, grabbing his hefty belly. "This is no illusion."

Mom patted his stomach affectionately. "You love my cooking, don't ya, Dingo."

Dingo. She had a pet name for him.

Another thing I hated.

"You cook now, Mom?" I asked, amazed.

"I've always cooked, dear. Just not as well as your father, so I never did much. I sew now too. Don't I, Dingo?"

Dr. Askers turned around and slapped his hand on his rump. There was a patch on the backside of his pants. The patch had little tulips on it and looked as if it had been cut from an old bedsheet.

"That's no iron-on patch either," Mom said proudly. "That's hand-sewn, every damn stitch."

The stitching was atrocious, zigzagging all over, each stitch a different size. "Betsy Ross you ain't, Mom."

She looked startled, as if I'd just cussed at her. Certainly she was aware that she wasn't any good. Nevertheless, I felt bad. But she brightened just as quickly and shrugged. "Not yet. But Betsy couldn't throw pots like your ol' mom."

She gave me a tour of her half of the garage, where she kept her pottery wheel and kiln. The shelves were neatly stacked with jars of glaze. Some of her plates and vases and figurines were scattered about her work bench in various stages of being finished.

"What happened to your painting?" I asked as I examined one of her vases.

"I don't know. We got here and I just didn't feel like painting. This island, the people, I don't know how to explain it, it made me want to dig my hands in the mud. *Feel the land*, you know?"

"Uh-oh, you're having a drug flashback to the sixties, Mom."

She mussed my hair and kissed me on the forehead. "Smart-ass punk, that's what I raised."

After lunch Dr. Askers took me out to the garage to see his work. As we were walking out of the house I caught a secret look pass between him and Mom. It was that old get-to-know-him, make-friends-with-the-boy look. I felt hurt that Mom was conspiring behind my back.

There was an old rattling refrigerator in the garage. Dr. Askers opened the door and took out a bottle of Budweiser beer. "Want one?" he asked.

"I don't drink." Not strictly true—I'd been known to guzzle a beer or two in my day. I just didn't want to drink with him, let him think this little game was going to work. I didn't mind being polite, but I wasn't going to be his buddy.

He shrugged and closed the refrigerator. He flopped down in a beat-up raggedy easy chair and started drinking his beer.

"I thought you were going to show me your work," I said.

"Look around. It's everywhere."

There were some large objects covered with torn paint-smeared sheets. I went over to one and pulled up the sheet. It was a life-sized sculpture of a man looking impatiently at his watch. He was dressed in a fancy suit and an enormous bow tie. In one hand were his car keys for a Mercedes, in the other hand were two tickets to a Broadway theater. The expression on his face was incredibly lifelike. He looked as if he was two minutes from murdering someone.

"I call it *Man Waiting for Theater Date*. What do you think?"

"Sounds sexist."

"That's what your mother says. But do you like it?"

Actually, it was good. But I didn't say anything. I just shrugged.

See, Dr. Askers had been building quite a reputation for his art during the last year. I'd seen his name in magazines, complete with photos of his sculptures. *Newsweek* praised his work "as neorealism with wit and intelligence, yet not giving in to fashionable cynicism." Since coming to Hawaii he'd been doing a series of pieces called "People Accidentally Met in Hell." I guess this guy staring at his watch was one of them. I remember that *Newsweek* article had a quote from him. The reporter had asked him why he'd started this series about people in hell after he'd moved to Hawaii. And he'd said, "Because only from the shores of Paradise can you recognize the depths of Hell." Dad had laughed at that quote when I'd read it as if he thought it was real witty. Didra and I agreed it was stupid.

I flipped up another sheet. A bunch of plaster people stood in a line behind a counter. A sign on the counter said DMV. The clerk behind the counter was talking on the phone, smiling. I don't know how, but somehow you could tell from the clerk's aloof smile that he was enjoying ignoring these people. That having them wait made his personal phone call all the more exciting, made his life more important. Like he was stealing their souls or something. The people looked defeated, tired, but accepting that there was nothing they could do but wait. That life was too much for them to have any other kind of response. A cold shiver scraped my spine.

I was getting into this now. It was like strolling through a wax museum, but better. I walked over to another sheet, but Dr. Askers waved me off. "Not that one, Eric. Not yet."

I dropped the edge of the sheet. "I have a question, Dr. Askers." Now that Mom wasn't here, there was no need to keep up the pretense of calling him Tom.

"Shoot, Mr. Marlowe."

"I've been reading about you in magazines. They say you're selling this stuff for good money."

"Very good money."

"Then how come you're still teaching at that dumpy community college we passed. Place looks like it's been bombed."

Dr. Askers drained the beer bottle, held it up to the light, then drank the last few drops. He flipped the bottle into a nearby trash can. It hit something hard and smashed. "I teach because I'm a teacher. Same as your dad."

"But Dad needs the money. You don't."

"I teach because I'm a teacher. I sculpt because I'm a sculptor. I eat meat because I'm a carnivore. I love your mother because I'm a man. Money never enters into these equations."

I had the feeling I was getting some warmed-over hippie-dippy crap from the sixties. I also wondered what was under the sheet he didn't want me to see.

During my week on Kauai, Mom showed me a lot of sights: Waimea Canyon, Olu Pua Garden, Hanapepe Lookout. We went snorkeling at Poipu Beach. Mom had learned to surf since moving here and she tried to show me how. But I just kept wiping out. It's not as easy as it looks in the movies.

Mom was pretty good though and people along the beach—locals, I mean, not tourists—would wave at her and say hello. She seemed to have a million friends. Back in D.C. she had a lot of friends, too, but they were all at the university.

We were sitting on the beach after about an hour of me getting washed off the surfboard. Her hair was lighter than in D.C. The sun had tanned her face, making those fine wrinkles bracketing her eyes and mouth deeper and more visible. She didn't seem to mind.

"How's Didra?" she asked.

"Great. She graduates next month."

"Good." Pause. "I take it you two are being careful."

I looked at her. "You mean sex?"

"Yes. Sex. You know how to be responsible, don't you?"

"Yes, Mom." I didn't really want to have this conversation. As usual, Mom took my reluctance to mean that I subconsciously wanted to talk about it. She tried to encourage me.

"We can talk about this if you want. You know you can ask me anything about sex."

"I can? Okay, then. Why does the female scorpion devour the male after intercourse?"

Mom tossed some sand on my chest. "You'll be glad for my advice someday."

"Maybe. But not today."

"You send me your plays. You let me read your plays. That's personal."

"Talking about writing with your mother is not the same as talking about sex, okay?"

"Honestly, Chip, sometimes you're so anal retentive."

Did I mention that Mom was once a psychology major? Until she and a girlfriend found out there were nude male models in the drawing class.

"You're such a good writer, Eric. I loved what you sent last week."

"You're my mother, you're required by law to say that."

"That's true."

We stared out at the ocean for a couple of minutes, watching some kids surfing. One kid just sat astride his board, waiting. Other kids would paddle in front of each wave and ride awhile, then paddle back out. He just waited, as if he were awaiting that one perfect wave. Nothing less would be worth the effort.

"You miss us, Mom?" I asked suddenly, though I'd sworn

to myself every day that I wouldn't ask such a little-kid question.

She shielded her eyes from the sun so that she could look at me better. "I miss you every minute of every day, Chipmunk. You can doubt that the sun exists, but never doubt that I love you more than anything."

"I know you love me. But do you miss us? Not just me. Us. Dad and me. Our family."

She looked out over the ocean. "I miss your dad. I miss you. I miss all the great times we had together. I miss our family. I was thinking about something the other day." She laughed and shook her head. "Remember the sink in your father's and my bathroom? How it would always get clogged up with fingernail clippings and hair and toothpaste?"

"You're making me sick, Mom."

"Your father and I used to argue about whose turn it was to clean the drain. I remember once he cleaned it and saved the hair, measured it with a ruler to prove it was mine doing all the damage." She sighed. "I miss that too."

Two little kids ran by shaking their wet heads. The cold water splashed against my hot skin. It felt good. Mom laughed. "You used to do that after you came out of the shower. You were three, I think. You'd shake your head real fast and splatter water on the bathroom mirror. Sometimes you'd make yourself dizzy and fall down."

"I don't remember."

"Be glad. What you don't remember, you don't miss." She stood up and toweled the sand from her legs. "Your dad and I are never going to get together again, Eric. We still love each other, though. We always will."

"People are always saying stuff like that. But they still split up."

"Love isn't always enough."

"I think I've heard that line on those Afterschool Special shows about divorce."

"It's still true, Eric. Sometimes life can be bad theater. You'll see."

"Bullshit!" I said.

She looked at me with surprise. I think that was the first time she ever heard me cuss. She laughed. "Bullshit back at you," she said.

We didn't talk about it anymore. In fact, we hardly said anything on the way back to the Jeep or on the drive home.

My last night there we went out to dinner for seafood. Mom and Dr. Askers offered to take me to a movie afterward, but I didn't feel like it. I wanted to get back and pack. My lost suitcase still hadn't arrived, but Mom had bought me a bunch of new clothes. So I packed those.

After I was done packing, Mom pulled out a stack of photo albums she and Dr. Askers had started since they'd moved here. Each photo was mounted on a single page and had a date printed under it.

"We take one photograph every day," Mom explained. "Sometimes we walk for hours just for that one shot."

"It's more fun looking for the shot than actually taking it," Dr. Askers said, chuckling.

There were photos of plants, buildings, local people, tourists, Mom throwing pots, Dr. Askers stirring white gunk, animals, birds, the ocean, leaves, a few things I couldn't identify. After a while, I realized something. There were none of Dad. None of me. These were the memories of a life that didn't include us.

When I'd finished looking at all the albums, Dr. Askers

took me out to the garage. This had been a nightly ritual. He offered me a beer, I refused, he plopped in his chair, I sat on a bench or leaned against the wall. We talked about nothing, the stars or the history of the island. He knew a lot about that stuff and it was pretty interesting, though I was careful not to show any interest.

"When are you going to let me peek at that one," I said, pointing to the covered sculpture he hadn't let me see.

"When you're ready."

"What's that supposed to mean? Is it dirty?"

"Art is never dirty. Let's just say it's provocative."

"I can take it."

He laughed and took a swig of beer. "*I* can't take it."

I wandered over to my mom's half of the garage. I picked up a platter dish she'd made. It was blue with oval swirls. Scattered throughout the blue swirls were pinpoints of white. It looked like the Milky Way. I stared at it for a long time. Finally, I asked, "Is she any good?"

"Who?"

"Mom."

"Any good?" He turned toward me, puzzled. "As a cook, artist, lover, friend, wife? What?"

"Artist."

Dr. Askers stared at me a moment, sizing me up. "Ordinarily I'd answer that with of course, she's terrific. But I have a feeling that's not going to cut it with you, Eric." He flipped the beer bottle into the trash even though it was still half full. "Truth? She's adequate. She can copy techniques, mimic style. But she can't do anything fresh, creative, original. She has no vision." He stood up, walked toward me. He took the plate from my hands and examined it as if it were an ancient artifact we'd just dug up at an old Indian burial site. "Vision is everything, Eric. To see not what is there, but what might be there. Not what is, but what could be. My first wife had vision. You remember Valerie?"

I nodded. They'd been divorced for three years. I remembered she had very nice legs, but the skin on her fingers was always peeling from scrubbing off the paint.

He smiled, put the plate down. "Valerie had the sight, man. The true sight. And she was a better artist than I am. Still is. But she didn't have the drive. Your dad has vision and he's smarter than I am." He turned and looked at me, the smile gone. "But I have more passion, more desire. That's the edge, Eric. The thing that gets the job done, that makes the vision not just an idea, but a reality. Passion. Lots of people have great ideas. They see something and say, 'Oh, I had that same idea before them.' But having an idea, thinking great thoughts, is not enough. You have to have the courage and passion to translate an idea into something concrete. Something that exists. Most people can't do that. That's why your mother calls me Dingo. Like an Australian wild dog, I find my prey and don't give up until I've hunted it down and defeated it in battle." He gestured at the half dozen sheet-covered figures. "Those are my trophies of battle. Like a soldier's scars or a sailor's tattoos. A vision made real so others can see what I see."

He went to the refrigerator and took out another beer. Again he offered one to me, again I refused. He twisted off the cap and drank. This was unusual, the first time I'd seen him take a second beer.

"I've read your plays, Eric. At least the scenes that you send to your mother."

My face hardened. I was torn. Mom had no right to show them to him, yet now that she had, I was curious about his opinion. Not that I'd ever ask.

"You have vision, too, Eric. I can see it in your words.

And you have the desire. The passion." He looked me straight in the eye, his face grim. "But you're hiding, Eric. Don't be afraid of it. Don't be afraid of passion." He kept staring at me, as if he were searching my face for something. "You understand?"

I nodded, but I didn't really care. I hated that kind of mystic garbage.

That night I couldn't sleep. I lay in bed and stared up at the big ceiling fan swooshing overhead. All the bedrooms had ceiling fans and the windows didn't have glass, they had thick wooden shutters that could be adjusted to let air in. I'd never been in a house before that didn't have glass windows, and even though it was no big deal, it still made me feel uneasy. As if I'd entered a looking-glass world where all the rules were different. It's like that dream I get sometimes since I started acting in school plays: I'm shoved on stage in the middle of a production with a thousand people in the audience. Only, I don't recognize the play, don't know what my part is, or any of my lines. I read somewhere that this is a common dream among actors.

I thought about what Dr. Dingo had said about vision and passion. Mostly it confused me. I had the feeling he was trying to tell me something about myself, but what? That I had the vision? To see what? That I had the passion, but I was afraid of it? I didn't get it. More Mod Squad nonsense.

The fan spun lazily overhead. I tried to focus on one blade and follow its course. But I kept losing it.

I thought about being home tomorrow. Dad would be at the airport waiting. I smiled thinking about that. It made me feel good knowing he'd be there. That the world would be back to normal.

I'd miss Mom. I'd even miss her meals, which, despite what Dr. Askers said, were still awful. He may have vision and passion, but he sure lacked good taste in food. I'd even miss the new smell of Mom, the scent of clay and glaze in her hair.

Dr. Askers. Tom. Dingo. This surprised me: I'd even miss him. Those evenings when we sat in the garage. He swigged a beer. We talked. Not about anything in particular. Politics. Something in the news. Local gossip. Thinking back, he was pretty smart. There were plenty of times I wanted to laugh at something he'd said, but I wouldn't let myself. When I played fair with him, he was a nice guy. I liked him.

Admitting that made me feel miserable—like a traitor to Dad. I mean, this was the guy who stole my mother away from my father. Stole her from our family. The same as if he'd sneaked through a window and shot her dead. How could I like him? This place was warping my judgment.

I got up and slipped into my jeans. It was warm enough that I didn't need a shirt or shoes. I tiptoed down the hallway and out the front door. The garage doors were padlocked to prevent theft of his sculptures, which according to what I'd read were worth $25,000 to $50,000 each, depending upon how many people were in each piece. I went in through the side door, which was unlocked because the pieces were too big to fit through. I pulled the cord on the overhead lights.

The usual pieces were lined up against the wall, hiding under sheets. They had to sit for a couple of weeks, then get another coat of whatever it was he put on them, then sit for another couple of weeks and get another coat. This went on with each work for three months. He was conscientious, I had to give him that. The only piece that wasn't covered was the one he was working on now. I'd watched him come out here every day and labor on it, staring, sculpting, applying his secret white gunk, filing and chipping at each face until it looked incredibly real. He was a chubby man, but he moved around that piece like a ballet dancer. When he was done, his face and beard would be spattered with hunks of white paste. He would be dripping with sweat. I thought about what he'd said about his being like a hunter attacking his prey. Well, with his face spattered like that and the sweat glistening on his skin, he did look a little like he'd bitten into a fresh kill, only instead of bleeding red blood, it spurted white paste.

I walked around his new work. It was part of his people-in-hell series. There were two couples, one older than the other. The younger man was pouring wine into the older man's glass. The younger man was laughing so hysterically that his face was contorted into something verging on grotesque. He reminded me of the Joker in Batman comics. The younger woman—his wife I assumed from her wedding ring, which matched his—was smiling, too, but it was a forced smile. Actually, she was glancing at her husband out of the corner of her eye and you could tell she was more embarrassed than happy. The older woman was chuckling politely, but she looked bored, as if she'd been through this kind of dinner a billion times. The older man, however, was laughing heartily, though not with the ferocity of the younger man. You could tell, don't ask me how, that he was being flattered and he was enjoying it. The title of the piece was etched on their plaster table cloth: TAKING THE BOSS TO DINNER.

I kept walking around it, studying the details. The faces were so human it was spooky. I half expected one of them to come to life. Mom would come out here in the morning looking for me, only I'd be a plaster waiter frozen in mid-service, handing them the check.

Around and around I circled, like the fan blade in my room. The hands, the clothes, a mole on one man's neck, a pearl necklace, a class ring, the leftovers on the plates. Everything so real. How did he do it? Maybe I hadn't understood everything he'd said to me earlier that evening, but standing there staring at this incredible work, I understood this much: he did have the vision. Orbiting the work as I was, I could see through his eyes for a moment. See what I might never have seen on my own. Suddenly I wished he were here so that I could ask him a thousand questions. Questions I could have been asking all along, but hadn't.

I was ready. Ready to see the work he hadn't wanted me to see. I approached it slowly, a little frightened, I guess. Okay, I admit that I kept looking over my shoulder to make sure those laughing diners weren't following me.

I took hold of the hem of the sheet. It felt a little damp from the humidity. I tried to guess what the figure was. All I could tell was that it was one person and he or she was sitting down. What was this person's hell? I wondered.

I paced backward, each step dragging the sheet off the figure. Finally it was undraped. It was a boy, but his back was to me. He was sitting in a school desk; you know, the kind you can only slide into from one side. The kind with an armrest for the right arm, the kind left-handers are always complaining about.

I grinned. Yeah, school. That was hell. No matter how good your grades were, how popular you were, it was hell.

I walked toward the piece, moving at an arc so that I could approach it from the front. As I came alongside it, I could see that this wasn't just a kid in school. This was something out of Freddy Krueger's *Elm Street* nightmares. Mr. Kreuger's Neighborhood.

The boy wasn't just sitting at the desk, he was being held captive there. The desk had armrests going down the right and the left side, so he couldn't slide out. He would have to climb out. However, there were hands coming out of the desk seat that gripped his thighs and wouldn't let him move. They were a woman's hands. A third woman's hand stuck out of the desk top and had hold of the boy's head. Her fingers were digging into the kid's face, pulling his head down toward the desk top. Even from a distance I could see her pointed fingernails slicing into his skin.

Neat, I thought.

I walked closer, approaching now from the front. The odd thing was that the kid didn't seem to be putting up much of a fight. If it were me, I'd be kicking and screaming.

Piled on the kid's desk were a stack of books. The titles were plain on their spines: *Complete Plays of Shakespeare, Our Town* by Thornton Wilder, *The Secret Sharer* by Joseph Conrad, *The Misanthrope* by Molière. I recognized all the works from my own classes at school. Except for the story by Conrad, they were all plays. That struck me as a little odd.

I could see as I got closer that the woman's hand grabbing the boy's face didn't come out of the desk, it came out of the books. The top book was open—it was *The Secret Sharer*—and the hand seemed to shoot straight out, as if opening the book had been like opening Pandora's box. Or a door to hell.

I stood in front of it now, close enough to touch it, though I didn't. Next to the stack of books was a big, juicy apple. Only, sticking out of the apple was a fat worm. It was the size of a worm, but as I bent closer I could see that it was really a snake, each crosshatched scale carved individually on its body. A menacing diamond pattern writhed along its back. But the face of the snake, though fanged and everything like all other snakes, looked somehow human. Like it was smiling. This is weird, but the face looked a little like Dr. Askers.

I touched the apple. It was so smooth, just the right size and shape. I touched the books' spines. I'd read these books and I knew instantly they were the exact right thickness. I touched the woman's hand spidered over the boy's face. The hand was slender and delicate, each finger long and graceful, even in its gruesome violence.

Then I touched the boy's head. The wavy hair. The jawline. It felt so familiar. My mouth went dry. I stooped down, peered past the woman's fingers to see the features on the boy's face. I recognized him immediately.

It was me.

My face.

I can't really describe how I felt at that moment. I'm not sure I even remember. Most of the next few minutes were kind of hazy, like I was sleepwalking.

Anyway, I do know that I ran over to the trash can with the white gunk, grabbed the canoe paddle leaning against it, and swung that paddle at the boy's head for a home run. The head and woman's hand smashed. I swung again. And again. And again. I guess this is what it's like to go berserk and murder someone, like in those teenage Satan cults I read about. White powder puffed up all around me from the smashed plaster. I started to sneeze. But I kept hacking at the statue like I was chopping wood.

Then two arms swung around me, hugging me tight. I

thought at first it was Dr. Askers, and I spun around ready to punch his Dingo lights out. But it was Mom. She was crying.

"Eric," she sputtered. "Oh, Eric." She seemed to want to say more, but all she could do was keep saying my name. She looked over her shoulder for help. Dr. Askers was leaning against the refrigerator. He was staring without any expression.

"My God, Eric," Mom said. "Do you know what you've done?"

I walked away from her. She must have known about the sculpture, she must have seen it while he was working on it. She had to have known it was my face. That meant she agreed with whatever sick vision Dr. Askers had. She had betrayed me, sold out to the enemy.

"I'll pay for it," I said, looking her in the eye.

"Damn right you will," Dr. Askers said. But he didn't sound angry. Just making casual conversation. "That baby would have gone for $25,000."

I swallowed, my senses returning, my perspective clearer. Twenty-five thousand dollars!

"That's a buck a week for . . ." He calculated for a couple of seconds. "Four hundred and eighty years. And a few odd weeks. I'll expect to see that dollar bill every week in your letters to your mother."

I could tell he meant it. That made me even angrier, as if he didn't take me seriously. What I'd just done wasn't a reaction to a fresh pimple. It wasn't because of a bad mood, a teen prank, an adolescent act of vandalism. It was because . . .

I hadn't figured that part out yet.

"Eric, why did you do this?" Mom asked.

Even if I wasn't sure, I had to give some answer. "He used my face. He had no goddamn right."

"It's just a sculpture. Like the *Mona Lisa* is a painting. Thousands of people would have viewed this work. You think Mona Lisa would have destroyed Da Vinci's painting because it was her face?"

"She posed for the painting. I didn't. He stole my face. He stole it and attached it to that monstrosity."

"Damn it, Eric, just because you didn't like it, that gave you no right—"

"Well, he had no right to—"

Dr. Askers blew an ear-piercing whistle. "This isn't getting us anywhere. Let me talk to him, hon," he said to my mom.

She hesitated.

"You're not my father, so we don't need any father-son chats," I said.

"This isn't father to son. This is artist to artist."

Mom left the garage, closing the door behind her. I noticed for the first time that she was wearing only a pajama top, which hung to her knees. Dr. Askers was wearing the matching pajama bottoms. Another thing to add to my list of things I hated about him.

With Mom gone, Dr. Askers patted his bare belly, which was big and furry as a bearskin rug and hung out over the elastic waistband. "I take it you didn't like my work."

I didn't say anything.

"You're a tough critic, Eric. Usually the artist takes the beating, not the work."

"I'm starting a new trend."

He opened the refrigerator and took out a bottle of beer. "Have one?"

"I'm underage," I said. "It's illegal to offer alcohol to a minor."

He chuckled. "I won't tell if you don't."

He carried the bottle over to me and held it out until I took it. I held it, but I didn't open it.

"You just twist the cap off," he explained, opening his bottle.

"I know how."

"Oh? Do you need help then? They can be hard to twist off sometimes."

I twisted mine off with a quick flick. "There. Satisfied?"

He drank from his bottle, smacked his lips, and smiled. "Hmmm, man. That's good stuff." He gestured at me. "Go ahead, try it. It's not too strong."

I tilted the bottle back into my mouth and began to gulp. I just kept gulping, not stopping to breathe or anything. It was sliding down my throat so fast I couldn't even taste it. I thought I'd gag toward the end, but I managed to choke down the whole bottle. When I was done, I tossed the empty bottle into the trash. It shattered.

"Happy?" I said.

He was grinning, and that's when it hit me. A thick belch pushed up my throat. That's when the flavor of what I'd just swallowed filled my mouth. Not alcohol. Not beer.

Cream soda.

I smacked my lips and made a face. "Jesus!"

"Good, huh?" he said. "Friend of mine owns a bottling company. He sends me a few cases every month. Paying off a piece I did for him."

"What's the point?" I said. "Just buy cream soda."

He laughed. "That would be logical, Eric. But I like drinking beer."

"So drink beer."

"I can't. I'm an alcoholic. Recovering. Sober for two years, three months, and sixteen days."

I shrugged. That didn't change anything. "Did my mother know that when she married you?"

"Yes. Your parents knew me before I stopped drinking. Your father was the one who talked me into entering a clinic. He took me to my first AA meeting."

"And this is how you repay him. Stealing his wife."

"You can't steal a person, Eric. People don't belong to anyone."

That was almost exactly what my father had said and it made me even madder. "You could have kept away from us. From our family. From my mother."

"We were friends. We still are. I loved your mother as a friend for years before we realized it had become something else. I think your father realized it before either of us did."

"If Dad had known, he would have stopped you!" I insisted.

"I guess you don't know your father as well as you think." He sighed and stroked his beard. "There was a time when I wished he had. But your dad knows there are some things that you just can't control. They just happen."

I didn't want to talk about this anymore. I looked over at the rubble of plaster and wire, the broken hands and head, the chipped apple with worm/snake. I didn't know what the thing was supposed to mean, I just knew I didn't like it. "So you're an alcoholic. You drink cream soda out of beer bottles because you like beer. But no matter how much you make believe, it's still just cream soda. It's not real."

He shrugged. "Who's to say what's real?"

"That's bullshit."

"Is it? A bunch of chicken wire and paste sent you into a rage. Does that make any sense? Is that logical? Is that real? Just chicken wire and paste." He walked over to a roll of chicken wire. He held it up. "Here. How does this make you feel?"

"It doesn't," I said.

He walked over to the trash can and pried off the lid. He tipped the can so I could see the thick white paste. "How's this make you feel? Angry?"

"No."

"Then what happened? You saw these same things earlier and you went berserk. What's the difference?"

"I don't know," I said. "Leave me the fuck alone."

He went to the refrigerator and tossed me another bottle. "Drink up, partner. There's nothing like a cold beer on a hot night, is there?"

I stared at him a moment. Man, he was the strangest guy I'd ever known. All these years he'd been coming over to our house and I'd liked him okay, but I'd never really known him.

I tossed the bottle back to him. "It's not beer, no matter how much you wish it was. The only thing for real is that by wishing it was beer it still makes you a drunk, doesn't it?"

The next morning when I checked in for my flight home, the woman behind the counter handed me my missing suitcase.

"This just came in on that flight," she said, pointing to the plane on the runway.

"Isn't that the plane I'm leaving on?" I asked.

She nodded.

I hugged Mom good-bye and she kissed me on each cheek. She wasn't crying, but I could tell she would once I'd gone. She wasn't still angry at me, but she was sad for me.

Worse, she had that guilty hangdog look, as if she were blaming herself for what I'd done.

"I'm sorry, Mom. You know, about last night. Batting practice."

She shrugged. "That's the past. Sometimes we feel things we can't put words to, but you have to express that feeling somehow. Like when you get this song going through your head over and over and you keep singing it, even if you don't like it."

"Mom, I love you, but stick with the plates and pots. Psychology's come a long way since the primal scream."

She hugged me again and laughed. "Like I said, smart-ass punk."

I shook Dr. Askers's hand. I didn't want to, but I figured it was the least I could do.

"You're welcome here any time, Eric," he said.

I knew that he meant it too. I thought about Dad, who'd be waiting for me at the airport. How would I tell him about what happened? Would all of this make any more sense to me on the flight home than it did now?

"Oh, yeah," Dr. Askers said. "This is for you." He handed me a cardboard box. It wasn't wrapped, so I started to pull open the flaps. He stopped me. "Open it on the plane."

"Thanks, Mom. Thanks, Tom."

"Don't thank me," Mom said. "This is the first I heard about this gift."

"Artist to artist," Dr. Askers said.

I thought about handing it back to him. I didn't need anything he had to give me. Especially that line of bullcrap about vision and passion he'd dumped on me last night. But I'd already hurt Mom enough for one trip.

"Well, thanks," I said unenthusiastically.

"Don't forget." He grinned. "A buck a week."

*　　*　　*

We were somewhere over California when I finally opened the damned box. It was the chipped plaster apple with the worm/snake poking out. Was this some kind of joke?

"That's very nice," the old man in the seat next to me said. "I used to be a jeweler and I know fine things."

So I gave it to him.

20 ～

"Wake up, wake uuuuuup, darlin' Cora/Gotta see you one mo' time. . . ."

The voice boomed loud enough to shake me awake.

"What . . . ?" Didra stirred beside me.

"Coz de sheriff and his hound dogs are comin'/Gotta move on down the line. . . ."

"Jesus," I said, sitting up. I rubbed my eyes. I'd been dreaming, I couldn't remember about what, but I knew it had been horrible. Some rabid animal with big teeth was chasing me. I was just happy to be awake. I whipped off the quilt and climbed out of bed. My knee ached where I'd banged it wrestling with Griffin. It looked a little swollen.

"What's going on?" Didra asked, squinting from the bright sunlight cutting across the bed.

"I think he's crazy. I really do."

Didra propped herself up on her elbows and yawned. The covers slid down over her chest. I turned away, not out of any gentlemanly instincts, but because seeing her this way only made me want her more. And that part of our relationship was over. I quickly pulled my jeans on.

"*Well, I whooped dat man, darlin' Cora/He fell right where he stood/Don't know if I wuz right, darlin' Cora/But, Lord, it sure felt good. . . .*"

"I thought he was supposed to be gone by now," Didra said.

"He is. I'll check it out." I started for the door, limping the first few steps, until my knee warmed up. But something bothered me. I mean, last night Didra did this big dog and pony show to keep Griffin here so that she could interview him. Now she wanted him gone as much as I did. I don't know why that bothered me. Not that I felt sorry for Griffin. It was impossible to think of him as having been used or taken advantage of. If anyone was a user, it was Griffin Coyle. Everyone else was a usee.

I caught a glimpse of Didra in the mirror as I marched toward the bedroom door. She was stretching, her arms sticking straight up like TV antennae. The quilt was bunched up around her waist. From the waist up, she was naked. My stomach went queasy as I thought of what it was going to be like without her in my life. Maybe I was making a mistake here. Maybe I just should have made love with her. Proved to her that I was better for her than that newscaster's son. I could *do* something. Fight for her instead of resign myself to the situation. I could go back to the bed right now, climb in, and we could make love all morning. Even if we did split up, I'd still have that to remember.

But my feet just kept limping out the door.

I closed the bedroom door behind me. The image of Didra stretching, her blond hair mussed, her eyes sleepy, her skin bone white, bleached by the sunlight, glowed in my mind like an apparition. I guess this is what a vision is like when those people claim to have seen Jesus or Mary or Elvis.

"Well, I'd rather drink muddy water/And sleep in a hollowed-out log/Than to hang around in this ol' town/And be treated like a dirty dog. . . ."

I followed the bellowing voice through the house into the kitchen. That's where I found Griffin, leaning back on a chair, his bare feet propped up on the kitchen table. He wore nothing but his underpants. He was alternately singing and munching on an English muffin piled impossibly high with half a jar of blueberry jam.

"Little energy loading," he said while he chewed. "Today's the big hunt, bwana. It's gonna be great. There'll be dogs and Jeeps and pickup trucks with gun racks, Thermos bottles with hot coffee spiked with a little whiskey, walkie-talkies, shotguns . . ." He winked and laughed. "Yes, sir, it's gonna be the biggest damn manhunt of the century." He got up and went to the kitchen window, peering out through the woods. "I imagine you'll be able to hear some of the dogs yelping from here. Maybe hear a shot or two. What do you think?"

"Get dressed. You're losing your head start."

He stared at me a moment. He'd restitched his forehead, but there were still some small scabs around the wound. Finally he shook his head and grinned. "You're pretty touchy this morning. Guess that means you didn't get any last night."

I felt like taking a swing at him. But just wanting to bothered me. I've hardly ever been in a fight, except for a couple seasons on the wrestling team. There was never any reason. I'd always been popular, got along with everybody. Sometimes one of the school outcasts would mumble something snide in passing about "the bigshot" or "Mr. All-American" or "President of the Student Pussy Council." But they never hung around to push the point. Even the mutants knew there was a line they didn't want to cross. It was one thing to be kind of an outlaw at school, which brought a certain distant respect. But it was entirely another to do something that would result in being shunned. So actual fistfighting rarely came up once I'd entered junior high school. But since I'd known Griffin, I'd already fought him twice and now I was clenching my fist, wanting to take another swing at him. And I didn't even know why. After all, he was right about last night with Didra.

Griffin walked slowly into the living room, singing loudly: *"Wake up, wake uuuup, darlin' Cora. . . ."*

I followed right behind him and stood guard as he climbed into his torn jeans and shredded shirt.

"That's a slave song I was singing," he said, fastening his belt. " 'Darlin' Cora.' You know it?"

"I heard it somewhere, I think."

"Black kid I knew back at Wise Acres used to sing folk songs and spirituals all the time. Had an awful voice, but he played the guitar better than Tom Petty and he knew about a million songs. Besides, your standards erode a little on the inside. I guess on the outside he'd be just adequate. But we all loved to hear him sing."

Adequate. There was that word again. I took a deep breath and walked over to the fireplace. I started stacking logs for a fire. Not that we needed one; the morning sun was already heating the place pretty thoroughly. I just had to do something with my hands. Keep busy.

Adequate.

Adequate.

Why had I asked Dr. Askers whether my mom was any good or not? What difference did it make? I'd held the serv-

ing plate she'd made in my hands, the one with the swirling
blue galaxy and pinpoint stars, and I should have just been
happy that she'd made it. Rejoiced in the act of expression.
Instead I'd studied it. Examined it. Dissected it with my eyes.
Was it any good? Was it art? And I'd asked the last man I
should have asked.

One who'd tell me the truth.

My mother had spent her life praising every little crayon
doodle or smeared fingerpainting or birdhouse made out of
popsicle sticks that I ever concocted. Everything I did was
wonderful by her. A miracle of creation. Why couldn't I have
given her the same benefit of the doubt?

I had betrayed my mother by scrutinizing her talent. I
had betrayed my father by being friendly with the man who
had destroyed our family. Maybe I'd also betrayed Didra by
not understanding what she was going through. Who was
left for me to betray? At least I'd never liked Griffin, so I
couldn't possibly betray him.

"I smell food," Didra said groggily. She was dressed in
black jeans and a white turtleneck sweater. Her blond hair
was tied back into a ponytail.

"I toasted one of your muffins," Griffin said. "Hope you
don't mind."

"I just wish you'd made one for me. I'm starving." She
headed for the kitchen. "You want something, Eric? Eggs or
something?"

I wasn't hungry, but if I'd refused, it would have sounded
petulant. "Half a muffin, please."

"Okay." She went into the kitchen, the door swinging
shut behind her.

"*Half* a muffin?" Griffin said. "Didn't burn up too many
calories last night, huh?"

I scraped the wooden match along the box and touched

the flame to the crumpled newspaper stuffed under the logs. The date on the paper was three months old. Soon the flames hugged the wood.

Didra returned with a toasted English muffin smeared with jam. She ate half and I ate half.

Griffin finished tying his boots and stood up. "Well, as much as I hate to leave this cozy domestic scene, I have places to go, people to see." He pointed a finger at Didra. "Good luck with that video, Lois Lane. Make sure that bastard sheriff is exposed. Don't make me look bad."

"Take care," Didra said. She offered her hand and he shook it.

I didn't offer mine and he didn't offer his. He just looked at me, grinned, and reached for the front-door knob.

That's when we heard heavy tires crunching up the driveway.

"Jesus!" Griffin said, jumping back.

I went to the window and peeked through the shutters. A blue tow truck was pulling up next to my car.

"Tow truck," I said. "The sheriff sent him to fix my car."

Griffin swore and backed against the wall, out of sight.

I watched the mechanic get out of the truck. He walked slowly around my car, circling it once like it was a dead carcass he just happened upon and didn't know whether to bury it or eat it. Then he went over and opened the hood. He stared at the engine a moment, then slammed the hood down again. He took off his Atlanta Braves baseball cap, wiped his forehead with his sleeve, replaced his cap, and spit into the dirt. He kicked gravel on the spit.

When he looked up, he stared straight at the house, straight at me really, even though there was no possible way he could see me or even know that I was watching him. Yet his eyes seemed fixed on me, as if he were looking right into my eyes. Then he grinned. And as his lips parted I recognized the toothless expanse of gums. It was the same man I'd seen yesterday. The man with the Louisville Slugger.

21 ~

"You got problems, boy." He walked around and opened the hood of my car. We both looked in, though I didn't really know enough about cars to know what I was supposed to be looking for. He reached in and fingered a few cables, twisted this and that, poked here and there. "The engine's not so bad. Won't take more'n a couple hours to fix that up good as new. Goddamn Japs build a helluva engine, I gotta give 'em that much." He walked around to the smashed front fender. He kicked the tire. "This is where you got your butt in a wringer. Gonna take a whole day to get this wheel workin' so's it don't wobble like a drunken whore."

"Can you do it here?"

"Here?" He laughed, showing off his smooth wet gums where teeth used to grow. Actually, he was only missing the front three teeth on the top, though the rest of his teeth had grown in at awkward angles, twisted and misshapen like thorns on a briar bush. He was only about twenty-five, with a hard, wiry body, but his face looked older, as if it were decomposing at a more accelerated pace than the rest of him. "Boy, I can't do squat here. I'm gonna have to tow this baby back to the station and talk my cousin outta goin' huntin' for that escaped convict we got roamin' around these hills. Lonnie's all geared up to catch Griffin Coyle. There's a reward, you know. Sheriff offered $500."

"Figuring that you can talk your cousin into working on my car, when will it be ready to drive?"

He shrugged, removed his cap, wiped his forehead, stared up into the sun as if he were reading cosmic signs for an answer. "I guess Lonnie could use the sure money rather than the maybe money of catching Griff. Alimony makes a man real practical."

"So when will it be done?"

"Tomorrow afternoon."

"Great."

"Of course, I'm gonna have to charge you for towing both ways, and I'm gonna have to charge you time and half for labor, this being a weekend and all. And parts are naturally extra."

I looked at him. He smiled cockily, not caring that I knew he was ripping me off. I had no other choice and we both knew it. I had my automated teller card, but, according to the phone book in the cabin, there was no local branch of my bank in town. The closest was in Brandon, further down the road. I'd have to have Dad phone in his Visa card number.

"Fine," I said.

"I'll call you when it's ready."

"The phone's broken. Just drive it out. I'm not going anywhere."

He looked over my shoulder at the cabin. "Sheriff said

you was out here with that Lester girl. Guess you'll have something to do between now and then, huh? Nature walks and such." He chuckled lewdly.

"As a matter of fact," I said, "I'd appreciate it if you could give Ms. Lester a lift into town."

"You want me to take her into town?" He seemed incredulous.

"If you don't mind."

"Hell, boy, I don't mind if you don't."

I started back up to the cabin and he followed. I stopped and turned around. "I'll be right back," I said, not moving.

His face reddened a little around the cheeks, but he stayed put. "Yeah, right. I'll go ahead and hook up your car."

Inside the cabin I found Griffin sitting on the floor, leaning against the wall. Didra sat on the chair by the fire.

"What's going on?" Griffin asked.

"Nothing. He's just hooking up the car. He has to tow it back to town to work on it."

"Hope you got a written estimate. Bobby Hodges will charge you for the snot in his nose if you let him."

"I'm not exactly in a bargaining position. Unless you want to go out there and negotiate for me."

Griffin held up his hands in mock surrender. "Hey, just looking out for you. That's what blood brothers do."

I turned to Didra. "He said he'd give you a lift into town. You can call a taxi there to get to the airport."

She looked startled and maybe a little hurt. But there was no use in pretending that this weekend would get any better. Even with Griffin gone, we'd still have too much to deal with.

She got up from the chair, tossed the empty gum wrapper she'd been twisting into the fire. She went down the hallway to the bedroom. I could hear her packing her things.

I peeked out the shutter and saw Bobby Hodges attaching the T-bar to my car. He moved around the car very quickly, reminding me of Dr. Askers moving around his statues of People Accidentally Met in Hell. Perhaps toothless Bobby Hodges was the Picasso of tow-trucking, an artist in his own way. Better than adequate.

He grabbed the winch control and started hoisting the front end of my car off the ground.

"I'm ready," Didra said, reappearing. Her suitcase was in one hand, her briefcase in the other. She looked very professional.

I took her suitcase and opened the door. She nodded at Griffin on the way out. He was still sitting on the floor. He gave her a funny gladiator salute—fist pounded against heart then arm stuck straight out—as she walked by, and said, " 'Those who are about to die salute you.' "

I gave him a sharp look, but he just chuckled. Mostly I thought his jokes were for his own amusement.

Bobby Hodges was talking on his CB. When he saw us approach, he finished his conversation and got out of the truck. He took off his cap as we approached. He stared at Didra with awe. "Just spoke to my cousin Lonnie. Said he'd work on it for ya, but I had to promise him a bonus. He really had his heart set on huntin' Griff."

"How much of a bonus?" I asked.

He shrugged. "A hundred bucks."

"Fifty," I said, just because I was getting tired of being taken advantage of by everyone.

"I don't know. The reward on ol' Griff is five hundred bucks."

"Then let him hunt ol' Griff. Give me a minute to grab my stuff and you can take me back to town with you. I'll catch a bus back to D.C. and let my dad handle this."

I started walking toward the cabin. To tell you the truth, I wasn't sure if I was bluffing or not.

"Okay, fifty bucks," he said.

I turned around and walked back. "Didra Lester, this is Bobby Hodges."

"Hi," Didra said.

"Hi," Bobby said. Then he looked at me with a puzzled expression. "How'd you know my name?"

"Sheriff told us last night," I said quickly.

"Oh, yeah." He nodded. He took Didra's suitcase and slid it into the storage box behind the cab. "Be in town in twenty minutes. Smoother ride than a dang BMW."

"I appreciate the trouble," Didra said. She smiled at him and he looked like he would faint.

"No trouble 'tall, ma'am. I'll enjoy the company."

He held the door open for her and offered his hand to help her into the cab, but I stepped between them and offered my own hand. She took it and climbed into the truck. I stepped up on the metal running board. It seemed like we ought to say something. I just didn't know what.

"I'll write," she said.

"Me too."

"Will you?"

"Yes."

"See you at Christmas vacation."

"You're coming home then?"

"I'm planning on it."

I shrugged. "Plans change, though. Right?"

She smiled sadly, leaned over, and lightly kissed my lips. Over her shoulder I could see Bobby discreetly facing the windshield, but trying to glimpse us out of the corner of his eyes.

"I miss you already," she whispered.

I didn't know what I was feeling. I felt bad, that much I was sure of. But was it because we were splitting up, weren't splitting up, because she betrayed me or I betrayed her? Because she was leaving now or coming home for Christmas?

"Bye," I said. I climbed down and slammed the door.

"Be back with your car tomorrow," Bobby said as he pulled away.

I watched the truck dragging Dad's car and carrying my ex-girlfriend disappear down the driveway.

"Hell of a turn of events, eh?" Griffin said. He was leaning against the porch post.

I walked up the steps and past him without saying anything. Inside the cabin, I returned to tending the dying fire. I tried to make some plan on how I would kill time until tomorrow. Play records, I guess, listen to the radio. Read a book. The records were mostly Broadway musicals and Barbra Streisand, stuff like that. And the books, jeez, thousand-page biographies about people I didn't give a crap about. Maybe I could work on my play.

"Hey, man," Griffin said, leaping over the sofa and flopping down in a prone position. "Lighten up. It was inevitable, pal. You guys weren't as simpatico as you think. I mean, when it comes to sex, she's knocking off homers in the majors and you're still bunting in Little League."

My face burned. I tossed another log on the fire.

"She's a great kid and all, but she's too secular for you. You're more the spiritual type. Like a monk."

There it was again. Calling me a "spiritual type." I mean, what kind of juvenile delinquent goes around using phrases like that? I'd have expected a lot more four-letter-word descriptions of what he meant. But this made me even angrier.

"Just shut up," I said. "You'd better hit the road."

"Sure, in a minute. I just figured I owed you this little

guy-to-guy chat. Seeing how I'm a little more savvy to the ways of the world, especially with women." He grinned and winked.

"I don't want your advice," I said, standing up. That's pretty much the same thing I'd said to Dr. Askers when he wanted to talk to me artist to artist. "Now get the hell out of here."

"Whoa, bro. Temper, temper." He sat up and swung his legs around to the floor. "All I'm saying is, that's a girl with a lot of drive. She knows what she wants and she knows how to get it. She has priorities. And apparently this newscaster's son is one of them."

So he had listened at the door! Before, when I'd just suspected it, I wasn't bothered. But now I was outraged. I took an angry step toward him. "Just leave. Now!"

He smiled, amused. Which made me angrier.

I swore at him and told him again to leave.

He stood up. He was still smiling, but the smile was fixed on his face. He wasn't amused now. We were face-to-face, less than a foot from each other, our chests puffed out like cartoon Popeyes.

He swore at me.

I swore at him.

That went back and forth a few times until one of us, I'm not sure who, shoved the other. A couple of tentative shoves were exchanged along with a few more curses. Then the punching started.

I'm not sure who threw the first punch. Maybe me. I was angry enough. The results were flying fists that pummeled each other with remarkable damage. Fights in movies aren't anything like the real thing. For one thing, the sound of a fist hitting a jaw isn't as dramatic without sound effects. The real sound is more like a dull smack, as if you dropped a book on a thin carpet. And in the movies they throw a lot of fancy punches, hooks, crosses, uppercuts. Who's got time to do all that? You just flail a lot, hoping to connect. And in the movies there's a lot of stomach punching. Not in real fights. Mostly you aim for the head. I think that's because you hope to draw blood and scare the other guy into quitting.

So this was pretty much the classic fight. For the first minute, anyway, when I knocked Griffin to the floor. I wasn't even sure which punch did the damage, that's how angry I was. It was a lot like that time in Hawaii when I smashed the statue that had my face. I was surprised to see Griffin go down. I think I even looked behind him because I figured he must have tripped over a stool or something.

Griffin sat there staring at me, rubbing his jaw. Although he said nothing, I could tell from his eyes that he was terrifically angry now. Funny, most of my anger had dissipated when I saw him go down. Now he was the angry one. It was like I transferred all my passion to him in that punch.

He jumped up, then dropped into a boxer's crouch that looked pretty professional. I admit, I was nervous. Before, when I was blind with anger, I had just waded in swinging. Now I adopted his stance, figuring he must know something.

He feigned with his right, then pumped two sharp jabs into my nose. My eyes welled up with tears, not from the pain, which was considerable, just from the beating. Something trickled out my nostrils. I hoped it was just mucus.

During that hope, he struck my jaw with another jab, then fired a left hook and a right cross. My head snapped back and forth like a weather vane. I staggered a moment, thinking I should just tackle him and take my chances wrestling. That's when he buried his right fist into my stomach. I doubled over, gasping, unable to breathe. I wanted to just drop to the floor, but I fought against that.

He shook off his boxer's crouch and sat on the sofa. I was still in my bent-over contortion, sucking air. I must have resembled one of Dr. Askers's statues.

"There's no zone like the ozone, eh, Eric?" Griffin said, massaging his knuckles. "It's like there's some giant rip in Heaven. Who knows what kind of creatures can slip through such an opening? Angels or demons?"

"Aaaayyyyeeeee," I hollered and charged straight at him. I dove into him, catching him by surprise. My shoulder rammed his stomach and all the air whooshed out of him. I smelled blueberry jam. The impact of my charge sent the small sofa toppling over backward.

I wrapped my legs around his waist and applied a scissors hold. He pounded his fists into my thigh and calf, but I held tight.

"I'll kill you," he said.

"I'll kill you," I said.

I heard the unmistakable metallic sound of a shotgun being cocked. Then a deep voice said, "One move and I'll kill both of you."

22

"Hey, *Lonnie,*" Griffin said from the floor.

"Hey, Griff. How y'all doin?"

"Been better."

"I guess that's damn sure true."

Griffin started to get up and Lonnie swung his shotgun over so that it was pointing directly at his face.

"Don't be makin' me pull this trigger, Griff."

Griffin laughed. "You ain't gonna pull that trigger. What the hell do you care if I get away?"

"Hell, Griff, ain't you heard? Sheriff's put five hundred bucks up for your capture."

Griffin's face went rigid.

Lonnie pulled out a pack of Juicy Fruit gum from the breast pocket of his black sleeveless T-shirt. He had a face full of stubble and long, thin, dirty brown hair. He wore a black baseball cap jammed tight on his head. Yellow stitching on the cap said Road Warrior. He looked like he was trying hard to imitate Bruce Springsteen. He pulled the stick of gum from the pack with his teeth, and managed to unwrap the gum and get it into his mouth, still using only one hand and his teeth. Then he offered me a stick. I shook my head. He offered one to Griffin, who accepted.

"I like peppermint better," Griffin said.

"Me too. But the machine was out. Son of a bitch only comes around to fill the machine once a month. I keep telling him we run out of peppermint two weeks after he's gone. But he says it ain't worth his time to come around these parts more often." Lonnie shrugged. "You get used to the other flavors after a while." He nodded at me. "You got a bloody nose, kid."

"You've got no right to hold a gun on me," I said. "I'm not wanted for anything."

Lonnie smiled. He had all his teeth, though they were as mangled and twisted as his cousin's. He looked a few years younger than Bobby, about twenty-one. "Maybe, maybe not. According to Bobby, that car tire of yours was slashed with a sharp blade. He figured it was curious you never mentioned that to the sheriff or to him. Figured you just might have something to hide. So he radioed me to come out and take a look-see. I know Griff well enough to know he didn't kidnap you or nothing. So you had to be a whatyamacallit, an accessory. Might be a reward for you too. We'll have to wait and see what the sheriff says."

"You have no authority to hold me prisoner," I said. I wasn't sure whether I was more angry or scared. I just knew I didn't want a guy like Lonnie to be pointing a shotgun at me. I also didn't want to be arrested and have to explain all this to my father. Technically, I guess I really was an accessory. I did give him food and shelter, I did lie to the sheriff about his whereabouts. Suddenly I had a vision of being sentenced to Wise Acres right along with Griffin. We could end up cellmates, for God's sake.

"I'm making a citizen's arrest," Lonnie said formally, deepening his voice so that it sounded more official. "If you're innocent, the sheriff'll let you go. Meantime, let's get going."

He marched us out of the cabin toward his car, which he'd cleverly parked at the bottom of the drive so that we couldn't hear him approach.

"What about my stuff?" I said.

"Let the sheriff figure that out."

"Let me at least lock the cabin."

He did. I used the key Didra had sent me. Another thing I'd have to return. It occurred to me that Bobby and Lonnie must have known that Didra knew as much about all this as I did. But they probably thought that because she was a girl, she didn't understand the implications. With any luck, Didra might still be in town when we got there. Maybe she could call her father and he could apply a little pressure to get me out of this. But the more I thought about it, the more I didn't want to owe her father anything.

"Let's go, boys," Lonnie said, motioning with the shotgun.

Griffin led the way. "You still driving that Camaro?"

"Hey, man, great machine. Eat up anything on the road, outside of them Italian sports cars. I rebuilt this baby from scrap."

"Looks it," Griffin said.

It did look like a junk heap, with large sections coated with nothing more than primer paint. Dents and dings pocked the entire right side of the car.

"I don't care what she looks like on the outside, Griff.

Long as she kicks ass on the inside. You know what I'm sayin'?"

We were standing next to the car now and Lonnie looked confused. "Well, now, this is the tricky part. This is where the bad guys always screw up in the movies. I suppose the best way is for me to ride in the back while you two ride up front."

Griffin started for the driver's side. "You musta been hit in the head too many times during football practice, Lonnie."

"Whattaya mean?" Lonnie sounded offended.

"Haven't you seen those shows where the driver jams the gas pedal and says to the guy with the gun, 'Go ahead and shoot. We'll both be killed'?"

"Yeah." Lonnie tapped him on the shoulder with the shotgun. "We'll let your buddy drive. He seems a bit more sensible than you."

I started for the driver's side and Griffin walked back toward the passenger's side. Just as we passed each other, he shoved me hard. I was caught off-balance and stumbled backward into Lonnie. The shotgun roared and I felt a wicked burning in my side.

23 ⌒

"**Y**ou'll live," Griffin said. "Now help me tie him up."

"Jesus," I said. My shirt had a tear in it, and the edges of the tear were red with my blood. I pulled up my shirt. It didn't look serious, no worse than if a shark had bit my side.

"You gonna help me or what?" Griffin said.

He had Lonnie down on the ground and was using Lonnie's belt to cinch his hands behind his back. He tossed me the car keys he'd dug from Lonnie's pocket. "Look in the trunk. These boys got enough crap in their trunks to survive a nuclear winter."

I walked unsteadily to the trunk and opened it. Griffin had been right. There was canned food, beer, tools, medical kits, a couple of revolvers, a dog leash.

I handed the leash to Griffin, who promptly trussed Lonnie's feet.

"Hell, Griff," Lonnie said. "This ain't right. This ain't right at all."

"Sorry, Lon. But you know I'm not going back there if I can help it. You done time there."

Lonnie nodded thoughtfully. "Guess I can't fault you none there. Food wasn't too bad though. They still got that green Jell-O on Fridays?"

"Green as snot."

Lonnie laughed. "Yeah, but I liked it. Don't suppose you boys could give me a lift a little closer to town? Leave me out next to the main highway?"

"I don't suppose," Griffin said. "I'll be heading in a different direction."

"Not in this you won't," I said. I had the hood open and was poking around inside.

Griffin looked around and I pointed to the shotgun blast in the side of the car. The pellets had torn through the fender and peppered the engine. Oil was leaking, a bunch of cables were severed, and the battery was chewed up.

Griffin kicked the side of the car.

"Damn," Lonnie said. "Damn!" I thought he was going to cry.

Griffin picked Lonnie up and stuffed him in the backseat of the car. "Since Bobby sent you out here he'll know when you aren't back pretty soon to come out here looking for you."

"Yeah, Bobby takes care of me."

Griffin shut the doors of the car. He clutched my arm and pulled me away from the car so that Lonnie couldn't overhear us. "Better grab whatever you need. We've got to hit the trail right now."

"We? I'm not going with you. You nearly got me killed."

Griffin pulled me further away from the car. "Listen. I'm done fooling around with you. If you want to be this stupid, that's not my concern. But what do you think will happen when his cousin gets here?"

"They'll come looking for you."

"Before that."

I thought it over. "Nothing. I'll give myself up. I didn't do anything serious. They'll have to let me go."

Griffin laughed bitterly. "Yeah, that's what I used to think. Let me rain a little on your parade, Howdy Doody. First thing that's gonna happen is Bobby and Lonnie are gonna kick the crap out of you. Not for helping me, not even for what we did to Lonnie and his car. They're gonna do it because they always wanted to kick around a kid like you and now they got an excuse."

"I can take care of myself."

"I've noticed. You've got a banged-up knee, a bloody nose, a shotgun wound, a wrecked car, an ex-girlfriend, and a posse after you for aiding and abetting."

"All the result of you being here."

"I suppose I forced Didra to sleep with that news guy's son."

I clenched my fists, ready to start swinging again.

He held up his hands. "Okay, okay. Sorry. Let's say you manage to use your brilliant logic and reasoning abilities to dissuade Bobby and Lonnie from performing brain surgery on you with a pipe wrench. After all, they like a good logical argument as well as the next hick. So you go quietly with them to the sheriff. Now, he's in the middle of leading this manhunt for me while mentally composing his sermon for tomorrow's church meeting. By now the whole town knows some outside kid helped me get away from him. And he's got to get up in front of them tomorrow with that humiliation. Oh, he's not going to be feeling too charitable toward you,

Eric. I wouldn't be surprised if during a body search they didn't find a little bag of coke on you."

Griffin started for the cabin. "Do what you want, man. Only remember this piece of advice. When you get to Wise Acres, keep away from Mighty Joe Hogan. A tractor ran over his head when he was a baby and he ain't been right ever since. He's the one who came after me in the shower. When he hears you were with me, he may want to soap your back for you."

I watched him enter the cabin.

I didn't move. I couldn't move. This is what Dad would have called the "existential dilemma," a choice between two options, both of which suck. I knew Griffin was trying to scare me. I also knew that he had. Even if he was half right, things looked bad.

I breathed in a great gulp of air and limped toward the cabin.

24 〜

We *hiked through the woods* for almost three hours before I talked Griffin into taking a rest. We sat on a fallen log and ate some sandwiches we'd made before leaving the cabin. They tasted soggy.

"Nice fit," he said, tugging the shirt he was wearing. It was my spare, a plaid cotton job that Didra had given me for Christmas. I'd brought it along this weekend as a romantic gesture. He was also wearing my gray Levi's jeans, which fit him okay at the waist but were a little long at the legs. He had to roll the cuffs. Although we were about the same height, he was longer in the torso, shorter in the legs.

I chewed on my sandwich slowly, wanting to savor every minute of rest I could. My wounded side was okay once I washed off the blood. Just a nick really. But my knee was hurting something fierce. It felt as if someone had dismantled all the bones and reassembled them in the wrong order. "You have any idea where we're going?" I asked.

"Away from the bad guys."

I snorted. "I can't tell the players without a scorecard."

"You think *I'm* bad." He shook his head. "Boy, you really have fallen down a rabbit hole, haven't you?"

I hated it when he talked that way. Like a teacher or a guru or someone with all the answers. "Look, I just want to know where we're going."

He pointed into the woods. "We need a car and we need money."

"Is there a gas station over there we can knock over?"

He gave me a wounded look, the same as the one my mom gave me when I questioned her sewing skills. That surprised me. Suddenly between the two of us I was the insensitive lout.

"I just want to find a phone," I said.

"What for?"

"To make a call."

"Oh, right, call Daddy."

I didn't answer.

He laughed. "You think he can help? Man, let me smoke whatever you've been sucking on."

"He'll know what to do."

"How can he? He's not here. He doesn't understand the situation. Hell, *you* don't understand the situation. You think you're Richie Cunningham and this is goddamn *Happy Days.*" He chomped on his sandwich. Jam squeezed out of the English muffin onto his chin. He wiped it with his finger and licked it off. "He'd tell you to turn yourself in, right?"

"Probably."

"And that's the last he'd hear from you on this side of the electrified fence. Trust me, I know what I'm talking about. Unless you're hot for one of these." He pushed up his shirt-sleeve and stuck out his tattoo.

Turning myself in would be the logical choice here. Trust in the system. It must work. That's how it gets to be the system. Sure, there are flaws, as there are in everything human-made. Sometimes people slip through the cracks. People like Griffin. Not people like me.

"Let's go," he said, standing. "I can smell them coming."

We crouched at the edge of the woods and looked down the hill at the big white church. A smaller house stood next to the church. There were no lights on in either building.

The sun was drifting lazily toward the horizon. It would be dark in another hour.

"Stay behind me, but stay close," Griffin whispered, though there was no one around to hear.

"What are we doing?" I whispered back.

"Just stay behind me." He crept ahead, hunched over, walking crablike through the chest-high weeds that covered the hill from the edge of the woods to the church below. I imitated his walk and stayed close behind him. A couple hours earlier we'd actually heard the men in the posse shouting to each other. And the yelping of anxious dogs. It was the sound of those snarling dogs that really made this whole thing suddenly very real to me.

We slipped through the field of weeds like burglars. Odd thing was, even sneaking through a field of weeds made me feel better. Like I was actually doing something to save myself, that my actions would have a direct influence on my life. It was as if everything that had happened to me during my whole life had been the result of someone else's decisions, not mine. It didn't matter that they may have decided "right," that I reaped all kinds of benefits, that my life was

like Richie Cunningham's. In a weird way this was the first
time in a long time that I felt as if I had some real control
over my life. You think funny thoughts when you're on the
run, I guess.

We came to the edge of the weed field. The rest was the
lawn belonging to the house and the church. The lawn was
neatly trimmed. A strip of garden surrounded the house like
a moat, though the flowers were mostly gone by this time of
year.

Griffin walked past the house to the back of the church.
There were a couple of concrete steps that led to a back door.
He took them with one giant step and tried the doorknob. It
was locked.

"What are we doing here?" I asked.

"Shhh." He jumped down from the steps and went to the
huge oak tree that grew between the house and the church.
He reached up and grabbed one of the thin branches and
broke it off, quickly stripping the few leaves that were still
leftover from autumn. What was left looked like a stick for
roasting marshmallows. He hopped up the concrete steps
again, jammed the stick in the doorjamb, gave a couple
twists, and the door popped open.

"Hey, you broke the door," I said.

"This isn't elementary school. Neatness doesn't count."

He went inside. I followed.

"What are we doing here?" I asked. "This is crazy."

"Relax, dude."

The inside of the church was modest: a raised platform
with a podium, rows of hard wooden benches, an old upright piano, a large wooden cross on the wall behind the
podium, one stained-glass window. That was all. No statues
or crucifixes, silver chalices, gold candlestick holders. There
was something awesome in its simplicity, as if the people

worshiping here didn't need to prove anything. Their faith was enough.

Personally, I didn't have much of a religious background. My mother was born Jewish, but she'd been a practicing Buddhist for the past eight years, though she doesn't burn incense because of her sinus condition. That's not as weird as it sounds. Mostly it means she meditates a lot and treats people nice. Dad doesn't have any religion, though he knows just about everything there is to know about all of them, even some you've never heard of practiced by maybe three natives on some remote island in the Pacific. He never tried to influence any beliefs I wanted to hold. In fact, he never discussed them with me unless I brought them up. He and Mom agreed that I should experience all kinds of religions before I made up my own mind on any one. They sent me to a synagogue for a couple of years, then a Catholic church, a Unitarian church, a Methodist church, and a Quaker meetinghouse. Except for some of the rituals, they all seemed pretty much the same to me. A lot of well-meaning people trying to make sense of things. People not wanting to feel alone in the great cosmic swirl.

"This is crazy, man," I said again. "This is a church."

"This is smart. This is the last place they'd look for us. The reverend sheriff's own backyard."

I walked down the aisle and climbed up to the podium. I looked out over the empty benches and tried to imagine them filled with people all facing me, waiting to hear what I had to say next. It was scary. It was hard to think of Reverend/Sheriff Jim Forrest, the thin man with the scar on his cheek, addressing a congregation of people every week, explaining the meaning of the Bible. Then again, this was pretty much what my dad did every day at the university, stood up in front of a bunch of students and explained the thoughts of the greatest minds in history.

"*Jesus loves me, this I know,*" Griffin sang, then laughed. He sat down on the back bench.

"What's our next move, Mastermind?" I asked, clutching the podium.

"To sin no more." He didn't laugh that time; he just sighed and stretched out on the bench.

I walked back down the aisle between the benches and sat on the bench in front of him.

"We need a car and some money," he said. "But first we need to wait for dark. I don't know about you, but I could use some sleep."

"Sleep? Here? What if someone comes in?"

"No one will come in. Trust me."

"Yeah, right." I stretched out on the bench and stared up at the ceiling. White rafter beams crisscrossed below the roof. It reminded me of a barn.

I suppose I could have argued with Griffin, but to tell the truth, I was argued out. What was the point? He knew what he was doing and I didn't. I'd never run away from authority before. Why should I when they were always holding me up as an example? I pretended I was some lost hunter in a hostile jungle and Griffin was my loyal native guide.

I must have fallen asleep thinking that, because next thing I know I'm walking through some steamy jungle wearing an Indiana Jones hat. I can see Griffin directly ahead of me, guiding the way. For some reason he's wearing a turban and white Middle Eastern pants. He looks like a genie from a lamp. He keeps going faster and I can barely keep up with him. Soon I'm running just not to lose sight of him. My side aches, my knee is throbbing. Suddenly I come to a river and there's a giant scorpion sitting on the riverbank. I don't know how, but I'm certain that the giant scorpion is really Griffin. "There's no food on this side of the river," the scorpion tells me. "Cross over," I tell him. "I can't swim," he tells me. This all sounds familiar and I remember some parable my father once told me about a scorpion and a turtle. Same situation, no food, the scorpion wants to hitch a ride across the river on the turtle's back. The turtle says no way, because he's afraid the scorpion will sting him and kill him. "That would be stupid," the scorpion explains. "If I sting you, then I'll drown too." The turtle accepts this as logical and swims across the river with the scorpion on his back. Halfway across, the scorpion stings the turtle. As they are both drowning, the turtle asks, "Why did you do that? You'll die now too." The scorpion just said, "It's my nature. I can't change my nature."

So I knew all that. Yet when this giant scorpion asked me to swim across with him on my back, for some reason I couldn't explain, I said, "Sure, hop on."

Then I felt a sharp poke in my back. I was drowning.

Another sharp poke.

"Hey, kid. Hey."

I opened my eyes. A pretty girl stood over me. I recognized her face. The girl who'd been with the posse yesterday, the one who'd asked me questions at the gas station. She held a pocketknife in her right hand, the blade open and pointed at me. I remembered the pokes in my back and thought, My God, she's stabbed me. I reached around to feel for blood. There was none.

"What the hell are you doing here?" she asked.

I sat up and looked at the bench behind me. Griffin was gone.

25 ⌇

I *jumped up from the bench* to search for him, but I guess I was still a little wobbly, because I banged my wounded side on the bench in front of me. The explosion of pain caught me by surprise and I let out a groan. I looked down and saw some blood seeping through my shirt.

"What happened to you?" she asked.

"Nothing," I said. I nodded at her pocketknife. "You going to use that or what?"

"I'm not afraid to."

I believed her. I glanced around the church looking for Griffin. Maybe he was in the bathroom.

"Mind if I use the bathroom before you stab me to death?"

"Sure, as long as you don't mind me coming along."

"Look, this is all just a big misunderstanding. Really."

She took a step closer to me. It was dark outside and

the only light inside came from the bulb over the back door that Griffin and I had come through. The door was wide open. "You're that kid staying out with the Lester girl, aren't you?"

"Well, I was."

"Yeah, I heard. Good-looking girl."

She seemed to be smiling, but that could have just been a shadow caused by the dim light. She had long, dark hair, thick as wool. She wore a long-sleeved T-shirt with an orange quilted hunting vest over it. Her jeans looked like the same ones she had on yesterday. So did the boots.

She pointed her knife at my bloody shirt. "We'd better get you inside and take care of that." She turned around and walked toward the exit. I followed. She still kept her knife open and hanging at her side.

"Do you live here?" I asked.

"That's right," she said.

"Then the reverend, the sheriff, is your, uh . . ."

"Father."

I didn't know where Griffin was, but maybe I was better off without him after all. Maybe there was still some way to talk my way out of this. I don't usually lie, but if I was going to start, this seemed like the best time. On the way into the house I started telling her a story about how Didra and I were driving along and we got into a big fight. I even gave some of the dialogue. In a way it was like writing one of my plays. I explained how we'd been yelling so much we stopped the car. I gave more of our dialogue.

The girl just kept walking ahead of me, her knife hanging next to her thigh. We entered her house, the sheriff's house.

The inside of the house was as modest as the church. Furniture, a TV, a Radio Shack stereo. The dining room table was covered with books and papers and an old portable typewriter. We passed by the table and I caught a glimpse of the page in the typewriter. *Fellow congregants. Today I want us all to examine two lines from the Bible: "Many shall run to and fro, and knowledge shall be increased," and "Write the vision, and make it plain upon the tables, that he may run that readeth it." What do these two lines have in common except the word run . . . ?*

I quickened my step to keep up with the girl, who was now climbing the stairs. I continued my story about the great fight I had with Didra. "Well, finally she got so mad she just drove off and left me standing by the side of the road. I started looking for a phone, but this isn't exactly downtown D.C. Yours is the first house I came to. I thought there might be a pay phone in the church."

We were in a small bathroom upstairs. "Sit," she said. She pointed at the toilet.

I lowered the lid and sat down.

"Take off your shirt."

I did.

She examined the wound with an expert's eye. She shook her head. "Good thing it was Lonnie that shot you and not Bobby. Lonnie just loads his shotgun with bird shot." She put her knife on the bathroom sink and opened the cupboard under the sink and pulled out a bottle of hydrogen peroxide. She wadded up some toilet paper, soaked it with the peroxide, and clamped it against my skin. "Hold that," she said.

I did. I didn't say anything. Since everything I'd just told her was a lie and she obviously knew it, I figured there was no point in saying anything else.

She wasn't much of a talker either. She cleaned the wound and taped a gauze bandage to my side without saying anything. When she bent over me, her long hair fell over one eye like a stage curtain. But she seemed to see me all right.

When she finished, she stood up and clapped her hands once. "All done. Now, where's Griffin?"

"He took off," I said. "Left me sleeping in the church."

She shrugged as if the information didn't mean anything to her. She washed her hands in the sink.

"Aren't you going to phone your father?" I asked. "Tell the posse?"

"Why would I do that? I'm the one that helped him escape from Wise Acres. Didn't he tell you?"

"My name's Jojo," she said.

I hadn't noticed this before, but she had a little shock of white hair at the peak of her hairline. Just a dozen strands or so.

"Eric Marlowe," I said, shaking her hand. Her skin was cool and moist from the recent washing.

"Yeah, my dad told me."

I had a lot of questions, like, Why did she help Griffin escape? What was he to her? Would she help me escape too? "When's your father due home?"

"Not for hours. He took all the posse out to dinner. When Dad pays they eat for a long time."

"And your mother?"

"She's gone."

I didn't know whether "gone" meant dead, divorced, or just split. I didn't ask. "Maybe I should be going," I said.

She shrugged again and walked out of the bathroom. I followed her down the hall. She went into what I guessed was her bedroom. I didn't enter, I just stood in the doorway. She sat at her small desk and opened a school book. "You can hang around awhile if you want. Get some rest. I've gotta study for an English test Monday."

"You're studying on a Saturday for a test that isn't until Monday. That's impressive."

"I'm trying to get a scholarship. If I don't get one I'm going to have to commute to Brandon to go to the community college there. That's fifty miles each way."

"What are you going to major in?"

She started to say something, then caught herself. She looked away. "I don't know yet. I don't have to declare until my second year."

"What were you going to say? I can tell you were going to say something." I don't know why I was so curious, but I was. There was something about her. One minute she's supercapable, with a knife pointed at me or bandaging a gunshot, the next she's embarrassed about her college major. "You can tell me," I encouraged.

"I don't know. I was thinking poetry maybe."

"Do you write poems?"

She reached up and nervously tugged at the errant patch of white hairs. "I've written some."

"Could I read one?"

"They're not to show. They're just for me."

"I write a little too. Plays. Well, scenes mostly. I haven't actually finished a whole play. I always plan them out before I start, you know, a big outline that says everything that's going to happen. But once I get halfway through, my outlines never seem to make sense."

She laughed. "I don't plan my poems until they're done."

I laughed too. "I'll have to try that."

She looked me over, scrutinizing me like she suspected I was a Nazi spy infiltrating a POW camp. After a silent minute she opened a desk drawer and pulled out a thick red notebook. There must have been two hundred pages in it. She opened it carefully on the desk and began leafing through the pages, silently reading a few lines, then turning the page to the next poem. Finally she selected one. She popped open the notebook rings and carefully removed it. She handed it to me. I was surprised to find it typed. Most of the kids I know who write poetry write it in elaborate calligraphy, as if they wanted you to frame it instead of read it.

I sat on her narrow bed, which was jammed against the wall. I turned on the lamp on the bedside table. There was a Sony radio alarm clock, an algebra textbook, a hardback collection of poems by Richard Wilbur with about a dozen thumbnail-sized scraps of paper sticking out of the top to mark specific poems. I leaned against the wall.

Before I read the poem, I decided to keep a neutral expression on my face. That way if it was as awful as they usually are, I wouldn't hurt her feelings too much. Some of the typed words were crossed out and new ones were written in above them. They were written in different colors of ink or pencil, which suggested she'd polished this poem several different times since typing it. My face now frozen into position, I began to read.

INSIDE THE SUN

BY JOJO FORREST

Inside the sun
everyone is warmer than they would be
on their own,
and heads are bent back at the neck to allow
for distance. Everyone here is tired, or should be,
of talking about love and the things that always go
wrong. They prefer the adjusting of chairs
for more comfort and warmth. Everyone stares

at the empty
pool and for a moment they think of what
it might be
like to be that wet and always moving
toward edges, slapping at boundaries, caught
tight by a whole planet, yet always moving away,
moving against the odds.
The sun
has turned slightly and heads are rolling one

degree to the right.
No one is worried about cleaning
deposits or the plight
of baby seals. We are taking the cure
before the sickness this time, learning
to survive in all this heat, learning to endure
things that never change or grow within our
reach. We are learning to live inside a star.

Somewhere along the line, I lost my composed features. I read the poem again. And a third time. By then my jaw must have been sagging.

She reached for the poem and I handed it to her. She didn't ask what I thought or if it was any good. That didn't seem to matter to her.

"I went to D.C. last year on a field trip," she said. "You know, to see Congress and all that stuff. We stayed overnight at this motel. About thirty of us. I remember looking out the window of my room and seeing all these people sitting around the pool. Not the kids, adults mostly, businessmen I guess. There must've been a dozen of them. Only they never spoke and they never went in the pool. They just sat around it and kept moving their lounge chairs to get a better angle of the sun. It was like some tribal ritual or something. That's what this is about."

I nodded. I seemed incapable of speech. I didn't know if the poem was good or bad or just adequate. I didn't care. I just knew that it touched me somehow, that I felt as if I'd just glimpsed inside her head and saw the world through her eyes for a minute and that would change forever the way I saw with my own eyes.

"Your poem made me want to be a better writer," I said.

She looked startled by that response, but not disappointed. It was the highest compliment I could think of. She seemed to understand. She placed the poem back in her red notebook, clamping the rings together, and slid it back into her desk drawer. When she turned back to me her eyes were paler than before, almost colorless. "I'd like to read your plays sometime."

"Plays-in-progress. Scenes mostly."

"I'd like to read them."

"Sure. I'll send you some pages."

I sat up on the bed, suddenly uncomfortable sitting on her

bed in her bedroom noticing her eyes like that. "Does your father like your poems?"

"You know fathers. They like everything their little girls do. Mostly he likes that it rhymes."

Her answer surprised me. I guess from what Griffin had said about the man, I'd expected some cruel, daughter-beating maniac. But Jojo seemed genuinely fond of her father. Of course, why would I believe anything Griffin said in the first place? Besides, none of that was my business now. I had to come up with some plan to get me back home.

I'm not sure how it happened, but one second I'm thinking about getting back to D.C. and the next I'm kissing Jojo. I don't know who started it, but we were both doing it now. She was sitting beside me on her bed and our arms were wrapped around each other and I tasted her tongue in my mouth.

When we broke apart, she stood up and said, "I'll be right back." She went into the bathroom and closed the door. I wanted to read more of her poems, but I didn't want to invade her privacy. She came out of the bathroom and held out her hand to me. "We'd better wait in my brother's room. You can hear any approaching cars better."

I followed her, figuring she just wanted to change rooms so that we both could cool off. I didn't ask where her brother was because if he was due home, she'd have told me. Also, I was wondering why I could still feel her kiss generating heat through my body. It wasn't like any kiss I'd ever had before, not even from Didra.

We went next door into her brother's room. It was totally dark and she didn't bother flipping on the light switch. She sat down on the bed. I sat beside her. We kissed.

The rest just sort of happened.

26 ～

"**A**re you asleep?" she asked.

"No," I said, but I knew I must have been until she asked. I looked over at the bed table. The room was so dark all I could see was the green LED illumination from the clock. 6:53 P.M.

She sat up and a rush of cool air was sucked under the blanket. "I must have dozed off."

I could only see the outline of her face and body, but she looked gorgeous. I thought about her poem, about that line *We are learning to live inside a star.* That's how I felt right then, lying next to her, feeling the heat from her body buffer my skin. Like I'd just blasted off from earth and was consumed by the heat of a star.

"Lie down," I said softly.

She did. She nudged me with her hand, so I turned away from her. She began scratching my back lightly. She had short nails, but it felt wonderful. "You have nice skin," she said. "Lots of freckles."

"I went to a church once where a kid told me that freckles were a sign that God was allergic to me. The freckles showed that he sneezed on me when I was born."

"That's awful. You didn't believe him, did you?"

"Of course. She was the reverend's daughter."

"Well, I'm the reverend's daughter, too, and I say she's crazy. Who are you gonna believe?"

"You. She never scratched my back like this."

She dug her nails in and I arched my back. She laughed and went back to her gentle scratching.

"Question," she said.

"What?"

"Why do you write plays? I mean as opposed to stories or poems. It's kinda unusual to start off writing plays, isn't it?"

"I don't know if it's unusual. Then again, I don't know why I write plays. Well, scenes really. I still haven't actually finished a play."

"You will."

She sounded so sure that I thought she must know something I didn't. My intentions were good, but my talent apparently wasn't built for the long haul to completion.

"Why do you write poems?" I asked.

She stopped scratching my back and snuggled up against me, skin to skin. "Because they're short."

"Really? That's all?"

"Sure. Each one takes me about a month to finish, but then when I read them it only takes a couple of minutes. All that power and passion and thought in just a couple of minutes."

I thought about that for a minute. She had a way of putting things that was simple and clear and made perfect sense. It occurred to me then that that was why I wrote plays. Because it was life stripped to the bare essentials: dialogue and motion. The character says something or does something. That's all we see. Like Peeping Toms spying on the neighbors through their open blinds. We judge the characters solely on what we see and hear, not what they think. Of course, I had been such a bad judge of character lately. Maybe that meant I was a bad writer too.

Jojo got out of bed and stretched. She seemed completely unashamed of her nudity. She walked into the bathroom and closed the door. I wasn't sure whether she intended to come back to bed or not, but I figured it was probably best not to push my luck.

I fluffed a pillow behind my head and smiled. I'd come down to this backwoods place for a weekend of sex with Didra. All the elaborate plans we'd made, the preparation, the colored maps, the letters and phone calls. And how many times had I pictured what would happen, what it would be like. I'd even gotten kind of nervous, not sure how I'd stack up next to her old boyfriend. I'd kept a twenty-four-hour-a-day vigil on my skin, certain I'd break out like Vesuvius the night before I was to drive down. After all that, nothing happened. Then I meet Jojo, read a poem, and bang—no warning, no planning, no anxiety. We make love as if we'd been doing it together for years. I didn't know what to think.

I threw the covers off, got up, and made the bed. I started dressing.

While I was dressing I thought of something weird. About three months ago I came home from class at the university early. I'd been fighting off a cold for a couple of days and finally it got the better of me. I just wanted to crash in my room and sleep for a week. Anyway, I walked into the house and started shuffling down the hall toward my room, but my stomach started to rumble and I thought I was going to heave right there in the hall. I dashed into the bathroom next to my room and there was a naked woman drying herself off after a shower.

I remember my mouth thudding against my chest. I also remember being kind of slow to react. She was very attractive. "Sorry," I'd mumbled.

I don't know what I'd expected her to do, scream or something. But she'd just laughed and covered herself with Dad's bath towel. "Hi, Eric," she'd said, thrusting her hand at me. "I'm Maggie Barnett."

I think I'd just lowered my eyes, shook her hand, and backed out of the room. Dad was waiting for me in the hallway. He had his bathrobe on.

"You okay, son?" he'd asked.

I was knocked out by that, because he'd seemed really concerned about me, not embarrassed about my finding this naked woman in the bathroom. I'd explained I wasn't feeling too well.

"We'll let Maggie take a look at you," he'd said. "She's a physician at the university."

I went to my room and climbed into bed. Maggie and Dad appeared a few minutes later, dressed. Maggie sat on the bed and held her hand to my forehead. "Bit of a switch," she said with a faint English accent.

"What is?" I asked.

"Having the doctor get undressed instead of the patient." She laughed in such a way that I had to laugh too.

Later that evening Dad brought me dinner. "Eat up, there's a fat apple pie waiting for you in the refrigerator."

"Are you dating Dr. Barnett, Dad?"

"Gee, son, dating is a strong word. If you don't tell Eddie

and the gang down at the malt shop, I'll let you in on a secret. Maggie and I are going steady."

"I hope you're practicing safe sex."

He didn't respond. Dad is not the kind to joke or brag about sex when it concerns a particular person. I guess it's old-fashioned, but I kind of like that about him.

"How long have you been seeing her, Dad?"

"Six months."

I imagined all these afternoon trysts while I was out at school. It was weird thinking about this naked doctor roaming around our house, standing nude in front of the same mirror I used.

I had mixed feelings. I was happy for Dad because he wasn't as lonely as I'd thought. But I was sad because this seemed like the final nail in the coffin concerning Mom playing a return engagement, familywise.

What was odd about the whole situation was that Dad hadn't told me about Dr. Barnett. I guess even Dad had his secrets.

When Jojo came out of the bathroom she looked at me buttoning my shirt. She didn't say anything until I'd tucked the shirttail into my jeans. "You have a nice body."

"You too," I said.

"You play sports at your school?"

"I used to wrestle some. Now I play basketball."

"What position?"

"Center mostly."

"My brother was a big football star. All-American. Had his picture in the paper more than a dozen times, I guess. Set a couple of state records."

"I'm not setting any records. Except for most chokes in a season."

She gave me a puzzled look, so I explained. I told her about my indomitable play during practice but my complete inability to score in a real game. She didn't comment on it, didn't say she was sorry or that it was a phase or any of those stupid things. She just nodded like it was a part of life, totally unexceptional. Somehow that made me feel better. I suddenly realized that I had told her all my secrets about basketball and writing. I no longer had any secrets. I didn't miss them.

She started dressing. "I just want you to know, this doesn't matter."

"What doesn't matter?"

"Whether we see each other again. I mean, that wasn't the point here, was it? It just happened."

I took hold of her bare shoulders as she buttoned her jeans. "I'd like to see you again." I didn't know I wanted to see her again until I'd actually said those words. But it was true. I started formulating plans for coming down here at Christmas vacation, or sending her a bus ticket to visit me and Dad.

She picked up her T-shirt from the chair and pulled it over her head. "Anyway, it was nice."

"I'm serious. I want to see more of you."

"You've seen about everything there is to see."

"You know what I mean."

She just looked at me, as if trying to decide how real I was being. All I knew was that I'd never felt more real.

I heard a car coming and quickly jumped into my shoes without bothering with socks. Jojo stayed calm, putting her finger to her lips. She walked over to the window and looked out at the narrow road that ran by the house and church.

The headlights from the car poured light on her and she shielded her eyes. Her hair was mussed, but it looked just fine. Then the light left her and wandered through the bedroom, illuminating high school pennants and photographs on the wall. I looked at one photograph, a husky boy in a football uniform frozen in mid-pass, his arm cocked back, his eye on the receiver. A little grin on his mouth because he knew there was no way he was going to throw anything but a perfect pass. I recognized the face.

"Jesus!" I ran over to the photograph.

"It's okay," Jojo said as the car passed on. "They're gone."

I grabbed the photograph from the wall. "This is your brother?"

"Yeah, that's Griff all right."

"Griffin Coyle is your brother?"

"Of course, didn't he tell you?"

"His last name is Coyle. Yours is Forrest."

"He had it changed. It was our mother's maiden name."

I just stood there clutching the photograph. The red hair was longer then and stuck out at odd angles from the blue-and-yellow football helmet. "He's your brother. Jesus."

"Yeah, he's my brother. What's the big deal?"

I looked around the room. This was his room, his bed we just slept in. Slept, hell, had sex in. I turned on the little light next to the bed so that I could examine the whole room. A couple of old wooden bookshelves bookended the door to the closet. I bent my head sideways to read the titles. *Alice's Adventures in Wonderland, The Catcher in the Rye, Stranger in a Strange Land, Adventures of Huckleberry Finn, Moby-Dick,* a lot of math books, physics, calculus, a couple of rows of science fiction.

"Interesting reading selection," I said.

"Oh, he's read a lot more than that. He's got boxes of

books out in the garage. All kinds of stuff, but mostly science and math. He loves math."

I dropped down on the bed, dazed. Griffin Coyle, the tattooed escaped convict I'd been on the run with, didn't seem to match the Griffin Forrest who'd grown up in this room.

Jojo sat beside me and held my hand. "He really didn't tell you anything, did he?"

I shook my head. "Just that the sheriff framed him. Wait a minute, then the sheriff is his father?"

"Yes."

"And his own father put up a $500 reward for him."

"He told you Papa framed him?"

"Yes. Isn't that what happened?"

She sighed and flopped back on the bed, her arms straight out from her body. "Griff, Griff, Griff . . ."

"What really happened?"

"What difference does it make?"

"I don't know. It just does. To me."

She looked at me and smiled sadly. "Yeah, he gets to you, doesn't he? Well, it's not a big, complicated story. The truth is Mama was a drunk, just like her mama and papa. Only, she went them one better and became a drug addict too. Mostly coke, some heroin, lots of crack. She ran around a lot as a kid, got pregnant when she was fifteen. She told us the kid died of pneumonia, but from some things she'd say when she was loaded, I think she sold him."

Jojo stared at the ceiling, her eyes blank, her face expressionless, as if she were telling a bedtime story to an infant. "Papa found her when she was eighteen; he was twenty-two. He'd just come here to take over the church when Reverend Anderson retired. Guess Papa figured he had enough power from the Lord to cure her, 'cause that's exactly what he did.

He made Mama his personal case and had her dried out within a year. Everyone says Mama was just fine after that, like a new woman. Friendly, funny, cheerful. She worked at the church on Sundays and everything. Then they got married. A year later they had Griff and a year after that they had me.

"I still remember the fun we had when I was little. Picnics and such at the river. We had this rope in a big ol' tree that hung out over the water. We'd swing out and drop into the river. Mama too. She got out the farthest. She'd even do somersaults and spins and bellyflops. She wasn't afraid of nothing."

I placed my hand on Jojo's arm, just to be touching her, offering some comfort. She didn't seem to notice me at all. I had the feeling that she would tell the story now whether anyone was in the room or not.

"I don't know when exactly, but it was some time around the time her own papa died that she started drinking again. Then taking drugs. She didn't speak to Grandma anymore."

"Why not?"

"From what I've been able to piece together, I guess when Grandpa got drunk back when Mama was young, he'd . . ." Jojo shrugged. "You know, molest her."

"Jesus."

"Anyway, Mama started in with the booze and drugs again."

"Surely your father must have known."

"He knew. He tried to help her. He sent her to clinics. He hired private nurses. He stayed home with her. He tried everything. Thing is, the more understanding and loving he was, the more it made Mama crave drugs and drink. I don't know why, it just was."

"What happened with Griffin?"

"Poor Griff. He was a straight A student, captain of the junior varsity football team; everything. It was like he could do no wrong. Like his life was laid out from birth to death on a yellow brick road of good fortune." She laughed. "When I was little I used to worship him. Then I hated him, how everything always went his way, how teachers always compared me with him. But something about Griffin, you couldn't hate him for long. He didn't rub anybody's nose in his luck, he didn't make you feel like you weren't as good as him. Mostly he seemed more surprised than anyone else when good things happened to him. You had to love him."

Apparently that wasn't the same Griffin I knew.

"Things changed for all of us as Mama got worse. She started sending Griff out for her drugs. He was young and she figured it was less risky if he got caught because he was just a juvenile. She knew Griff would never tell on her. He did it for a couple of years. By then he was captain of the varsity football team and had a scholarship to college. One day he just up and told her he wasn't helping her anymore. So she started sending me for the drugs. That's when the trouble started. Griff found out one day and took the drugs away from me. When we got home he told Mama that I wasn't buying for her anymore either. If she wanted her drugs she'd have to get them herself. He started flushing the coke I'd bought down the toilet. Mama went crazy. She started hitting and scratching Griff. He let her, but he didn't stop flushing the junk. That's when she got the gun and shot him."

"She shot her own son?" I gasped.

Jojo smiled sadly. "Well, the drugs made her do it. You just don't think straight." Her eyes looked out the window as if she were staring at a special star, as if she could see it up close the way no one, even with the fanciest telescope, has ever seen it before. Her own personal star. Then she looked at me. "He wasn't hurt too bad, but the shock of shooting Griff sent Mama into screaming fits. So Griff grabbed me and what was left of the drugs and we took off. He wanted to leave the state, go to California or something. But we didn't have any money. That's why he kept the drugs. Figured he could sell them and we'd have enough money to get away for good. Only he sold them to an undercover cop."

"Why not go to your dad?"

She shrugged. "Papa hadn't had much success with her so far. I guess Griff blamed him some for Mama's condition."

"For a golden boy, he sure had a trainload of bad luck all at once."

"Papa hired the best lawyers he could afford, tried awful hard to get Griff off. But Griff wasn't very cooperative. It was as if he wanted to get convicted, you know?"

"What about your mother?"

"She took off with some guy."

I let out a long stream of air. It was as if I'd held my breath for the past few minutes while she told me the story. Now that I could breathe, my chest felt tight, constricted. "I'm sorry," I said, needing to say something. "I wish he'd told me."

"Griff doesn't tell anybody anything. Not anymore. He's changed. It's like he doesn't care about anyone else. And that stupid tattoo. He treats it like a pet."

"But you helped him escape."

"He's still my brother."

"But your father is hunting him down," I said.

"My father is doing his job. It's killing him inside, but he's doing it because he believes that he has a public trust. A duty. But he loves Griff, even if Griff blames him for everything."

I got up from the bed and went to the window. I looked up into the sky and tried to find my own star. "Why does he call his bullet wound 'Walter'?"

"Does he?" She laughed without humor. "Walter is what Mama almost named Griff. After her father."

There was a long silence. Jojo closed her eyes for a while. I stared at the stars. When she spoke, her voice came from far away. "Why weren't we enough for Mama, Eric?"

"I don't know," I said. She nodded as if my answer explained the entire situation. She closed her eyes again.

I leaned against the window and felt the cool glass pressing my forehead. I felt exhausted, deflated. The tale of horror Jojo just told me made everything about my life seem petty and silly. I didn't want to think about it anymore, I just wanted to get back home.

"Miss me?" a male voice asked.

"Griff!" Jojo said with delight.

I turned. Griffin was standing in the doorway staring at me, his eyes angled with anger. A kitchen knife was clutched in his hand.

"So this is the thanks I get for bringing you to my home," he said. "You jump my sister's bones."

Then he started toward me.

"Griff!" Jojo shouted and leaped off the bed. She stood between him and me. "Don't do this."

I didn't move. Not out of fear, I didn't really feel any fear. I didn't feel anything. I was an observer, watching this drama unfold as if it were a play. If he stabbed me and I didn't like it, I could always rewrite that part. Yeah, I know it sounds crazy, but that's how I felt.

"How long have you been listening?" I asked. For some reason, having him know any of the personal secrets I'd told Jojo worried me more than his knife.

"Long enough," he said.

Then I realized he was just as upset at my knowing about his secrets as I was about his knowing mine. That's what this was all about.

"Screw it," Jojo said with frustration. "You want to kill him, then do it. But make it fair." She reached into her pocket and pulled out her pocketknife. She tossed it to me. "Go ahead, boys. I'm going downstairs for something to eat. The survivor can join me."

She walked out of the room without looking back.

27 ～

"There's one," Griffin whispered from the bushes. "Over there."

The car was parked in the driveway. I peeked over the bushes and looked the house over. The only light came from the second story. I heard the faint sound of a television, the theme song to some old show I couldn't remember. "It's clear," I said.

"Come on." He came out from behind the bushes and started for the car. I followed. It was an old gray Buick with more rust spots than paint. The car looked as if it were decomposing, just months away from the junk heap.

"You sure you know how to steal a car?" I asked.

"I learned in prison. You just smash the window, get inside, yank the ignition system with these pliers." He held up the backpack that contained the necessary tools. "Then we yank the ignition out and replace it with the one from the sheriff's truck, turn the key, and we drive off. Simple."

That's what Griffin had been doing when he left me in the church. He'd taken the ignition system from his father's truck, the one that hadn't worked in six months. Part of his master plan. We steal a car and drive out of the state. Only we'd had to walk three miles to the nearest house and their cars were locked in a garage with a security system. "People used to be more trusting," Griffin had complained as we walked the next two miles to this place.

We hadn't talked much during our walk. That was okay by me, because it gave me time to think about Jojo. The way she had just walked out of Griffin's room, leaving the two of us standing there with our knives. Somehow she'd made us feel pretty silly. I'd tossed the pocketknife on the bed and followed her out, saying to Griffin, "I'm hungrier than I am angry."

He didn't say anything, but he appeared at the kitchen table a few minutes later. Jojo cooked three omelets and we all ate every last bite.

Before Griffin and I left, I pulled Jojo aside to say good-bye. "I don't know what to say. This hasn't been the most traditional date."

"Yeah." She grinned. "I don't usually cook on my first date."

I kissed her.

She handed me a folded piece of paper. "Address and phone number. If you want."

"I want," I said. I was afraid to tell her how much I wanted. I stuffed the paper in my pocket.

She kissed me.

As Griffin and I had walked along what passed for a highway around here, I kept replaying the evening with her. I had come down here this weekend for romance after three months of planning, but I had found it with someone I'd just met. I shook my head and smiled.

"I hope this car has plenty of gas," I said as we approached it. "We don't even have enough money to fill the tank."

He didn't answer. He just kept walking. I thought about my father's gas credit card in the glove compartment of my car. Along with my condoms. All I had was about fifteen bucks in cash. But if we could get to a branch of my bank, I could use my ATM card for more.

Griffin walked around the car. "Looks like shit, but Mr. Carver's been driving this heap as long as I can remember."

"I just noticed something," I said. "How come you don't talk like you did before. Using all that slang and bad grammar."

He laughed. "I just talked the way you expected me to. You drove up yesterday in your daddy's car, saw me standing there in my numbered shirt. You had me figured out, right? Southern redneck, criminal. Right?"

I didn't say anything.

"Right?" he repeated.

"Let's get on with it," I said.

"Right." He opened the driver's door. It was unlocked. He slid in and removed the tools from his backpack. He went to work on the ignition system.

That's when I heard the screen door creak open. I looked up, and standing on the back porch was a tall, lanky old man with white hair. He wore old khaki pants and a thick black sweater. "Howdy, boys," he said.

Griffin jerked up so fast he hit his jaw on the steering wheel. "Hey, Mr. Carver," he said to the old man.

"That you, Griffin Forrest?"

"Yes, sir."

"Fixin' to steal my car, huh?"

"Yes, sir."

The old man nodded. "Well now, I guess you've had your troubles, boy, and an unfair shake here and there. But that don't mean I gotta give you my car, does it?"

"No, sir."

"You steal my car and I'll have to go inside and phone your daddy up and report it. But if you and your desperado friend here just keep moving on, well, then I guess I don't have to phone nobody about nothing."

Griffin didn't say anything. He just sat behind the wheel and looked ashamed. This was the first time I'd ever seen him look as if he doubted himself.

"Well," the old man said, scratching his white hair. "I'm missing my show. I'll peek out my window when I get upstairs. I'm hoping I don't see no wanted criminals." He went inside and closed the door.

Griffin quickly packed the tools and slid out of the car. "Let's get out of here," he said.

We walked for another four miles, passing three other houses along the way. But for one reason or another, none of the cars were stealable.

"This isn't getting us out of the county," I finally said. "Why don't we just hitchhike?"

"Because by now most of the people who live around here know about us. They're looking for us, so they can collect the reward."

"Except Mr. Carver."

Griffin smiled. "Mr. Carver was sheriff around here before the reverend. I used to do odd jobs for him."

I shook my head. "I don't understand this place or any of the people."

"From what I can tell, you don't understand people, period." Griffin left the side of the highway and waded through another field of weeds.

"Now what?" I said, but followed.

We came out the other end of the field and I could see all the lights from the town. We were only about a mile away.

"I thought we were supposed to be heading away from town," I said.

"We only have two options. Either we steal a car and drive the hell out of here, or we take a bus. The car stealing hasn't worked, so we try the bus."

"Won't your father be watching the terminal?"

"He's only one man. The rest of his little posse is probably pretty discouraged by now about finding me. Nobody's going to hang around Goodhart's Drugstore waiting for me to show up."

"Goodhart's Drugstore?"

"That's the bus terminal in this town."

"Convenient," I said. "We can drink cherry Cokes while we wait. Let's go."

"No point," he said. "They're closed. They won't open again until tomorrow morning."

"Tomorrow morning? What do we do until then?"

Griffin took his boot off, placed his hand inside the boot, and punched through the glass window. Glass tinkled to the floor inside. He slipped his boot back on his foot and tied it. "Come on, man," he waved at me.

I'd been keeping watch by the bicycle racks. The high

school was located on the edge of town and there weren't many houses around, so no one heard us breaking in.

"Hurry up," he said.

I jumped down into the cellar window well. Griffin had already opened the broken window and climbed through. It was dark, but there was enough light to tell we were in a locker room.

"Don't they have alarm systems here?" I said, thinking about the fancy electronic security system at my school.

"It's not keeping people out of school they gotta worry about around here. It's keeping them in." I couldn't make out Griffin's face in the dark, but I followed his dark shape between rows of lockers. He ran his fingertips along a wooden bench. "This is the girls' locker room. Boy, if these benches could talk."

I don't know how he found his way in the darkness, but he led us out of the locker room and up the stairs to the classrooms. The corridor floors were linoleum, but they were so old they were warped from the years of adolescent shoes marching the halls. Still, the floor was highly polished, as glossy as if it were brand-new.

"This where you went?" I asked. We were strolling down the hall, glancing in the classrooms.

"Yeah. My classmates will be graduating about the time I was supposed to be released from Wise Acres. A counselor said I could probably pass the high school equivalency test and graduate anyway. But I'd lose my scholarships. Seems the Ivy League schools don't like juvenile delinquent drug dealers at their schools."

"What do you plan to do? I mean, say everything goes our way and we get out of here."

He laughed. "That's important to you, isn't it? To know what the next move is. To have a plan."

"Hey, forget it. I don't want to know, okay."

We walked silently the entire length of the school. The bulletin boards were all decorated with Thanksgiving Day cutouts the students had made. Each bulletin board was the responsibility of a different class of tenth graders. The one I liked best came from Mr. Bentley's class. They were very big on 3-D effects.

Griffin stopped in front of the class display case of sports trophies. They had one dinky third-place trophy for basketball and a fourth-place silver plate for wrestling. All the rest were for football. And from the size and number of the trophies, they must have been quite a powerhouse in their division. There were team photos of the football teams from the last ten years on either side of the display case.

"Here's you," I said, pointing to last year's team. Griffin was listed as the quarterback. He had that same charmed grin as in the photo in his bedroom.

Griffin pushed through the auditorium doors without looking back.

"Wake up."

I opened my eyes. For a moment I didn't know where I was. I looked around, saw all the auditorium chairs. Was I in a play, did I fall asleep during rehearsal? I stood up, felt a little dizzy.

"Come on, bro. Time to make our great escape."

I stared at Griffin, my memory returning.

"No, it wasn't all just a bad dream," he said. "Now let's get out of here."

I followed him down the hall again. We passed a couple of pay phones and I had the urge to call Jojo, just to hear her voice, make sure she wasn't a dream either. I fished a quarter out of my pocket and deposited it in the phone slot.

"What the hell are you doing?" Griffin shouted from down the corridor. "I told you your dad can't help us here."

I took the wadded paper out of my pocket that Jojo had given me and unfolded it. It was a copy of her poem, "Inside the Sun." Above the title, written in large looping letters, was her address and phone number. I remembered the intricate, detailed map Didra had drawn for me, the tiny, precise handwriting. I thought about Didra in bed smoking. I smiled. I didn't know if Jojo smoked or drank or what. I didn't really care.

I dialed the number on the poem.

Griffin waited down the hall with a disgusted expression on his face. He still thought I was calling my dad.

"Hello?" a male answered. I immediately recognized the sheriff's voice.

I didn't know what to do, what to say. Should I ask to speak to Jojo? Would he recognize my voice? Maybe I could disguise it, filter it by talking through my shirttail or something.

"Hello?" he said again. Then, "Griff? Is that you, son?" The sadness and despair in his voice caught me by surprise. "Let me help you, son."

I hung up. My fingers were cold, my hand was trembling.

"So what's he say?" Griffin asked when I caught up with him. "Daddy going to come down to save his only son?"

"You were right," I said. "There's nothing he can do."

I walked out of the drugstore, keeping my head down so no one could get a good look at me. I kept walking around the block to the alley in back. Griffin was waiting there behind the garbage cans. He was doing push-ups as I approached.

"Bad news, Rambo," I said.

He kept doing his pushups.

"The fare to Brandon for two is $34.80. We only have $15.23."

He pushed up, lowered himself, pushed up. "How much for one to D.C.?"

The question caught me by surprise. "What makes you think I asked?"

He stopped his push-ups and stood up. He slapped his hands clean and smiled. "How much?"

"Thirty-one dollars."

"Either way, you come up short. Our only hope right now is to scrape up another twenty bucks so that we can take the bus to Brandon and get to your bank. I help you get there and you stake me a few bucks to get away. Deal?" He held out his hand.

"Let's just do it," I said, ignoring his hand. "Where do we get the twenty bucks?"

"Prayer." Then he laughed crazily until he had to lean on the garbage can for support.

The three kids were shooting baskets. The black kid was short, maybe 5'8", but he was sinking a lot of shots from around the key. One white kid was taller, my size or more. The other white kid was tall but overweight. They were about our age, playing one on one, the first to sink seven baskets won. The winner would stay in and the odd kid would then challenge in. They were fairly friendly, no one trying too hard on a hot day like this.

"What are we doing here?" I asked Griffin.

"Relax. You'll see."

We watched the game from behind some hedges that bordered the trailer park we were in. The basketball court belonged to the trailer park and consisted of one basket and a paved surface about the size of half a court. There were no painted lines on the surface, just some crooked chalk marks to indicate boundaries.

Griffin filled me in. "A few of the people who live here are old-timers, been here twenty years or more. Most of the residents are transients; come in to work the mines over in Crenshaw, but don't want their families over there. They don't keep up with the local gossip that much, so they don't know me."

"So? What do we do, break into their trailers and search for twenty dollars?"

He grinned and clapped me on the back. "If I thought we could get away with it, Eric, I would. But these people keep an eye on each other's stuff. Nope, we're gonna have to get that twenty dollars the old-fashioned way."

"Earn it?"

"Con it."

"Hey," Griffin said, as he approached the three kids.

They looked us over with unsmiling faces. I noticed now that the big clumsy kid wore a gold stud earring.

The black kid pivoted and fired the ball. It sunk through the hoop, rattling the chain net that hung from the rim. The tall white kid grabbed the ball, dribbled away from the board, turned, and hooked the ball over his shoulder. It swished through the hoop.

"You guys interested in a challenge match?" Griffin said. He smiled brightly.

"We're playing," the black kid said. He was wearing just nylon shorts and his Air Jordan sneakers. No shirt, no socks. The tall white kid had a sleeveless T-shirt on that was torn in the back. The heavy kid with the earring wore jeans and Keds.

"I'm talking a money game."

The tall white kid stopped dribbling and caught the ball. "How much?"

"Fifty bucks."

The black kid snorted. "We ain't got fifty bucks, man."

"How much you got?" Griffin asked.

"That's none of your business," the husky one said.

The white kid tossed the basketball to the black kid. "You gonna play us dressed like that?" He pointed at Griffin's heavy boots. I was wearing running shoes, which were terrible for basketball.

"Hell, we'll play buck naked if it'll make you feel better," Griffin said.

The black kid shook his head. "We're just shootin' around, man. We're not looking for a game."

Griffin laughed. "Tell you what. All three of you against my friend and me. That make you less scared?"

The tall white kid's face went hard. He was a good player and he didn't like being called scared. He nodded to his buddies. They huddled and conferred in low mumbles.

"This is crazy," I whispered to Griffin. "We only have fifteen bucks. Even if we win, we're still short for the bus tickets."

"Trust me, okay?"

"Like hell."

The kids broke up their conference. The tall white kid nodded at Griffin. "How much we talkin' about?"

"Well, there are three of you, so we'll put up fifteen dollars. Five dollars a man."

They exchanged looks. The black kid went over to the grass lawn that surrounded the court and opened his sports bag. He pulled out his wallet, counted out four singles and some change. He rooted through his bag, found another couple of coins. "Five bucks, man," he said.

The other two dug out their money.

Griffin looked at me and held out his hand.

"Are you some kind of basketball whiz?" I asked.

"No, you are."

That's when I realized just how long he'd been listening outside the bedroom while I told Jojo about my botched basketball career. "If you know that much, then you know I'm not very good in pressure situations. I choke."

"Then you choke." He shrugged. "We don't have a lot of options. Unless you want to go back to trying to steal a car."

I handed him my fifteen dollars.

Griffin turned to the three kids. "Okay, we've got five dollars for each of you, but you'll have to kick in an extra five."

"What for?" the tall kid asked.

"Because you have an extra guy. That makes it fair. Simple mathematics."

They looked confused, but began rummaging through their wallets and bags for another five dollars.

"I'll be right back," the tall kid said. He jogged off between two trailers and disappeared.

"Let's warm up," Griffin suggested.

We stripped off our shirts down to bare skin. I made a few lay-ups, then snapped the ball out to Griffin. He shot from about six feet away, but missed every shot. After he missed five times, I grabbed the ball and marched out to him. "Can't you play at all?" I whispered harshly.

"A little. Football's really my game."

"This isn't football."

"Don't worry," he said. "The fat kid's no good. We can block him out. The black kid is fast, but I'll guard him close, try to keep him from shooting. All you have to do is block the tall kid and outshoot him."

My stomach was already hurting. It was the same intestine twisting that went on before each game. I had to go to the bathroom, but there was no place to go. "Feed me a few," I said, and moved out to the key for some shots. I took ten shots. I made two.

The tall black kid laughed and whispered something to his fat friend. He guffawed like a walrus.

The white kid ran back with a five-dollar bill in his hand. "Let's do it, man."

The husky kid with the earring, who made a point of trying to look tough, held out his hand to Griffin. "I'll hold the money."

Griffin shook his head. "You hold your team's money. I'll hold mine."

"How about rechalking the boundaries," I said.

The black kid took out a huge piece of chalk and began tracing the lines. He drew a single horizontal line for the free throw key. "One game to ten, win by two. Winner's outs. Okay?"

Griffin looked at me. I nodded. "Okay," he said.

"Clear all changes of possession," I said.

"Of course," the tall kid said.

"Clear them to the back," I added. "Sides don't count."

"Sure."

"Shoot for outs?" the black kid asked. "Do or die."

"Go ahead," I said.

He walked to the free throw line, then backed up about three feet further away from the basket. "Okay?" he asked.

"That's about right." I nodded.

He shot the ball. It bounced off the rim, then dropped through.

"Our ball." He grinned.

Basketball isn't like any other sport. There's a flow to it that always verges on being out of control. It's like riding an unbroken horse, I guess, or driving a car at two hundred miles an hour. You think you're in control, but then suddenly everything changes and you're smashing into a wall and bursting into flames. A couple of months after the divorce, Dad took me on a canoe trip down the Susquehanna River in Pennsylvania. We hit some rapids and we had to paddle so hard that my arms went numb. See, when you're going down rapids in a canoe, the only way to maintain any control is to paddle faster than the current is carrying you. You slow down for a second, or think about something else, the whole canoe flips and you're dragged down the river. That's what basketball is like.

Griffin's plan worked pretty well at first. The three locals were a little tentative. They kept expecting us to quit toying with them and start doing some kind of Harlem Globetrotter number on them. When it occurred to them that we were playing as well as we could, the 1–1 tie quickly became 4–1, their favor.

I'd just missed another lay-up and the tall kid had

snatched the rebound out of Griffin's hands. Griffin called a time-out.

We walked to the other end of the court and sat on the grass. We were both sucking air.

"You weren't kidding," he said between wheezes. "You really do stink."

"Is this your idea of a pep talk?"

"It's reality therapy, baby. We need their money or you and I are going to spend some quality time together. In prison."

"You guys playing ball or playing with each other?" The husky kid with the earring sneered.

Griffin walked away from me without another word.

When the score was 7–3 he called another time-out.

"You want pep talk, I'll give you pep talk," he said, panting. He held up his hand until he'd gulped enough air that he could talk. "Think about what it feels like to have bars on the windows, to get strip-searched by guards who enjoy their work, to shower with your butt against the wall."

"I told you, I don't do well in pressure situations."

"You do well on tests, don't you?"

I nodded.

"You used to wrestle, right?"

"How'd you know?"

"Some of the moves you used when we fought. Were you any good?"

"I usually won."

"That's a pressure situation, isn't it?"

"Yes."

"So you do well on tests and you were a good wrestler. Those are pressure situations. But you suck during basketball games that count. Why?"

"If I knew, we'd be winning."

"I know why."

"Oh, really," I said. "And after only one session of analysis, Dr. Freud."

The black kid was at the other end of the court shooting. The tall kid hollered at us, "You guys give up?"

"I think they're kissing." The husky kid chuckled. Sweat glistened over his entire body.

"It's simple, Eric," Griffin said, walking away. "You're not a team player."

I watched him walk to the other end. I didn't follow. Not a team player! What the hell did that mean? I was president of my class, president of the student council, designated leader of every group that came along. But why? Because I paddled the ship faster than the current or because I just didn't rock the boat? Because I demonstrated qualities others admired and wanted to emulate? Or because I fit in so easily, so neatly. So adequately.

I walked back down the court. "What's the fucking score?"

I was dribbling, moving past the tall white kid, being picked up by the husky kid with the earring. He smelled bad, like fried tar. The longer he was out here sweating in the sun, the worse he smelled. I cut around him too.

As I'd walked down the court after our time-out, I'd thought of a dozen reasons why Griffin was wrong about me. I compiled a case built on logic and clear steps of reasoning. I had examples to support my suppositions. I could call witnesses, hundreds of witnesses, if the case made it to the Supreme Court.

Just one thing bothered me. If I was right, if I was part of this great team, then why did I never feel a part of them?

But I wasn't thinking about that as I dribbled around the fat kid. I was thinking about basketball. About the purity of movement, the feel of the ball grazing my fingertips as I dribbled, the strain on my hip as I suddenly changed direction, the burst of power from my legs as I leaped up into the air and scooped the ball over everyone's heads.

The ball plopped through the basket as I fell to earth.

Our 4 to their 7.

After that, things got rough.

I was boxed out by the tall kid and the husky kid. Griffin drove to the basket and made a lay-up. His first basket.

"Foul," the black kid said. "You were charging."

"Your feet weren't set," Griffin argued.

"They were too," the husky kid growled. "Charging."

"You had your back to the play," I said to him.

He cursed at me and I cursed back.

"Let's just take it over," the tall kid said.

"Like hell," Griffin said. "He moved into me. There was no charging."

"Do or die," the black kid said.

Griffin started to argue, but I grabbed the ball and marched to the spot about four feet behind the free throw line. I arched the ball. It dropped through.

"5 to 7," I said.

*   *   *

The black kid and the husky kid tried to intimidate me with a lot of body checks and waving their hands in my face. The tall kid played on pure talent. He wanted to win, but he wasn't thinking about the money, he was thinking about victory. That made him the most dangerous.

Griffin did a good job using football defense to keep the other two from me. That pretty much made it a one-on-one race between me and the tall kid. We were about the same height, but his reach was a little longer. But I was in better shape from practicing with the team and had a little more strategy.

They were leading 8–7 when Griffin stole the ball from the husky kid. The husky kid got so mad he shoved Griffin hard from behind and knocked him to the ground. The ball fell from his hands and the black kid picked it up and shot. The ball swished the metal net.

"Foul!" I cried.

"He tripped," the husky kid said with a snort.

"Do or die," I said, pointing at the husky kid.

"I made the basket," the black kid said. "I'll do or die."

Griffin got up from the pavement. His palms were scraped raw. Blood welled up from the shredded skin. "Shoot," he said calmly to the black kid. He smiled at him.

The black kid took the ball, but he didn't do any fancy dribbling as he walked to the spot to shoot. He just stood there for a long time, longer than last time, trying to concentrate. He shot.

The ball bounced up off the rim, hit the backboard, then fell to the side.

I took the ball. "Let's go."

*　　*　　*

Before the game was over, we had all been knocked to the ground, elbowed, shouldered, kneed, and gouged. Most of it came from them, especially the husky kid, who lumbered after us, wheezing, and hurled his body into ours out of desperation.

I was limping from a twisted ankle and Griffin's stitched forehead was bleeding again. My sore knee felt as if a porcupine were in there firing needles.

The last shot of the game was a hook shot over the shoulder that arched high over everybody's outstretched hands. Impossible to block. The ball sank with a resounding rattle of chains.

Griffin walked slowly toward me. I didn't move, because I was afraid my knee wouldn't support me and I'd fall to the ground. If I laid down at all, I knew I'd never get up again.

The tall kid came over to me and offered his hand. "Tough playing," he said.

"Thanks." I shook his hand. "You too."

"Who do you play for?"

"Potomac High in D.C."

He nodded. "I play for Crenshaw. Lotta jungle ball over there."

"Here too," I said.

He shrugged.

At the edge of the court, Griffin bent over and retrieved our shirts. He wearily handed me one of them; I wasn't even sure if it was the one I'd been wearing before. I put it on anyway, though I didn't bother buttoning it. He held his shirt in his hand and went over to the husky kid, who was collapsed on the grass sucking air like a bicycle pump.

"Money," Griffin said, holding out his hand.

The husky kid lifted his head and made a face. He lowered his head and closed his eyes.

"The money," Griffin repeated. "We're in a hurry."

"Best out of three, man," the black kid said.

"One game to ten," I said. "That's what we bet on."

"Best outta three," the husky kid said, standing up. He drew up his chest in a menacing manner.

"Give him the money, Ben," the tall kid said.

Ben, the husky kid, shook his head. "Best outta three."

Griffin threw his fist into the husky kid's stomach. It happened so fast that the rest of us just stood there and watched as Ben doubled over. His eyes bulged as he hugged his gut. Griffin hit him again, this time in the nose. Blood spurted from one nostril down over Ben's lip and chin. A red mucusy string dangled from his jaw. Griffin shoved him hard and he fell backward to the ground.

"Hey, man," the black kid said and started for Griffin.

"Cool it, Dennis," the tall kid said.

"Yeah, Dennis," Griffin said. He kneeled beside the moaning husky kid and frisked his pockets until he found the twenty dollars in bills and change. He slipped them into his own pants, which were soaking wet from sweat. He had to peel his pocket open to jam the money in.

He reached over and pulled Ben's gold stud earring off. "This is for interest."

"Let's go," I said.

Griffin smiled grimly at Ben, then walked away. We hurried out of there as fast as we could with our battered bodies. The black kid followed us part of the way, but we lost him down some alley.

We were staying pretty much to the alleys, working our way closer to the drugstore/bus terminal. When we got there, Griffin said, "Better let me buy the tickets."

"Aren't you afraid of being recognized?"

"I peeked in when we walked by this morning. Old man

Goodhart doesn't work on Sundays and I don't know the guy working there right now. So he can't know me."

I let him go, because I was happy for the chance to sit. I waited in the alley behind Goodhart's, sitting on the cold pavement, leaning up against the brick building. I smelled the garbage that lined the alley, but it didn't bother me. Sitting had never been such a glorious experience.

I didn't think about the miracle of winning, or how Griffin had battered that jerk Ben, or what our next step was going to be. I just sat. I breathed in rhythm with my throbbing knee.

"Let's go!" Griffin shouted, running down the alley. I wasn't alarmed at what was making him so excited, I merely marveled at his ability to still run.

"What?" I said slowly.

"Get up, let's go. The bus is leaving."

Somehow I ran. I wasn't conscious of it. It was like my mind was traveling piggyback on somebody that I didn't have any control over.

We shot out of the alley to the place where the buses parked. One bus was idling. A young mother and her toddler daughter were entering the bus. I could make out three other people inside, looking out the tinted glass at us as we ran.

The bus driver was closing the baggage compartment on the side as we ran up. He was a thin young man who wore his bus driver's cap at a rakish angle, like he thought he was a jet pilot or something. He was trying to grow a mustache, but his hair was too fine and blond for it to make much of an impression.

"Any luggage?" he asked, annoyed.

"None," Griffin said.

That seemed to cheer the driver up. "Well, let's go then, boys. I got a schedule to keep."

Griffin guided me ahead of him. He handed the bus driver the ticket while I slowly climbed the metal steps into the bus.

"One ticket to Washington, D.C.," the driver said, tearing off part of the ticket. He handed the rest of the ticket to me and started to climb in after me.

"Wait!" I stopped and turned around. "Isn't this the bus for Brandon?"

"Brandon's the other way, son. Your ticket says Washington, D.C., same as the front of this bus."

Griffin had backed away from the bus and was waving.

The driver started to push me ahead of him. "Don't worry none about the big city, son. Folks there aren't much different than anywhere else."

"Take care, dude." Griffin grinned, moving farther away from the bus.

I entered the bus the rest of the way and yanked down the first window I came to. "What about you?" I said to him.

He frowned, held his hand to his ear as if he couldn't hear me. The driver gunned the gas and the engine growled loudly. We began to pull away.

Griffin waved.

28

Home. The word had new meaning to me now. Everything was different. I was different. I had changed so much I wasn't sure Dad would even recognize me when I walked in the door.

I wondered how I would tell him about what happened. About Didra. About Jojo. About Griffin.

About his car.

The bus turned a corner and I looked out the gritty window. Griffin stopped waving and ducked down the alley behind Goodhart's Drugstore. He looked like some kind of gnome, all hunched over and sticking to the shadows of the building. Then he just vanished. Gone from my life as suddenly as he'd entered it. Tonight I would call Jojo and find out what happened. First, I would wire her some money and she could take it to wherever Griffin was hiding. I owed him that much, even if I didn't figure ever to see him again.

Funny, because I sort of missed him already. Without him, it was as if someone had turned down the volume on my life.

I sat back in my lumpy seat and watched the town slide by as if I were on some Disney World ride staring at a lifelike replica of a quaint little town, the kind they're always showing in movies, where everyone is everyone else's pal. Who were these people? How did I get here? All I'd wanted was a weekend of passion with Didra. But she was gone, too—back to school, back to her anchorman's son. I tried to feel bad, but I didn't. That surprised me most of all. Sure, I was excited about Jojo, but that didn't seem to have anything to do with how I felt about Didra. I guess with Didra I'd always felt as if she were just another of the undeserved gifts of my life, my lucky life in which I'd been rewarded for just being what people wanted me to be. With Jojo, nothing had been planned. The passion was real. She didn't know all the president-of-this, captain-of-that crap about me that seemed so important before. She just knew *me,* the guy who was scared and on the run. And that was good enough for her.

The bus took another corner and I saw Ben, the husky kid with the bloody nose, and the skinny black kid and another white kid, not the basketball player, about Ben's size marching toward downtown. They looked mean and anxious for a fight.

"*This is your driver, Mr. Drake,*" the p.a. system announced. "*The weather is clear and we should be in D.C. right on schedule. Your first rest stop will be in two hours at Ma Leary's Family Restaurant. Try their chicken-fried steak. Best in the South.*"

The bus came to a stop at the light and idled loudly. I looked back over my shoulder out the window. The three angry boys marched in cadence, like military police. Ben kicked the bumper of a Toyota as they passed it. It was all so dramatic, like a movie. It made me think about the little scenes I wrote, how I was never able write a whole play, never come up with an ending. Maybe it was because I didn't like the way things usually turned out in real life, all confusing and messed up, like with Mom and Dad and Dr. Askers. If I couldn't change the way life was, especially the way my life was, I didn't want to just pretend things were better than they were and write some phony happy ending where everyone sits around grinning at each other over vintage wine. I didn't want to lie.

Maybe that's why I never came through in the clutch before, never could make the shots in the real game. The game was stacked, the rules were bullshit. Our lives seemed so programmed to be this way or that, that if I made those shots I was just doing what was expected of me, what I'd been programmed to do. Like dating Didra. I'd never realized all this before. Thinking about it gave me a sharp pain behind my left eyeball, as if someone were twisting a corkscrew through it from inside my skull. I closed my eyes and rested my head on the seat. But these thoughts kept flapping at me like a flock of crows. Why had I played so well with Griffin? He'd said I wasn't a team player. What did that mean? An invisible crow pecked at my eye and suddenly I knew what Griffin had meant. I was a member of the team all right, but I didn't believe in what we were playing for. I didn't share the same goals as everyone else. They just thought I did and, because I kept getting rewarded for playing along, I believed I was part of the team. But that guy they all talked to, voted for, dated, passed the ball to—that wasn't me.

I felt kind of dizzy thinking about that. Because if I didn't belong with the team, where did I belong?

The light must have changed, because the bus grumbled into gear. Slowly we rolled forward through the intersection.

"Let me off!" I said, jumping up from my seat. "Stop the bus!" I ran up to the front of the bus and grabbed the railing. "You've got to let me off."

"There's a lavatory in the back if you feel sick," he said.

"Stop the damned bus!" I said.

I ran hard. My sore ankle buckled a little and my knee felt soggy, but I made pretty good time. I didn't know my way through the alleys, so I had to just follow the streets, backtracking where the bus had gone.

I didn't think about why I was doing this. I'd thought about so much sitting there on the bus. I knew I was somehow different, but I just didn't know how to put it into words yet. All I knew for sure was that this was the right thing for me to be doing. I guess it was like basketball, sometimes you just did it. I was paddling to beat the current.

He wasn't in the alley behind Goodhart's, but it didn't take me long to find him. The shouted curses and threats drew me to the next alley over, the one behind the movie theater.

When I entered the alley, Griffin was down on the ground and Ben and his big buddy were kicking at him. The black kid stood off to the side. He didn't look like he really wanted to be a part of this anymore.

As I ran, I snatched up one of the garbage can lids and held it like a shield. I let out a howl like an attacking Viking. Ben looked up with a startled expression. The new kid looked like an older brother, his face thick with the same dull eyes and slack mouth. The black kid was already running away.

Ben just stood there, as if he expected me to stop and

talk. I didn't. I just kept running until I plowed right into him, my shoulder tight against the garbage can lid. I smashed into him full force. He tumbled to the ground and I landed on top of him.

A heavy kick to my ribs lifted me off him and sent me rolling to the side. My hand was locked in the handle of the garbage can lid, so that came with me. Ben's brother followed me, leaping over his own prone brother so he could deliver another kick. He was cursing me through clenched teeth. Saliva sprayed from his mouth. I held up the lid as my shield, and he kicked the lid. He must have liked the feel or sound of it, because he kept kicking the lid over and over until the metal handle cut deep into my palm.

"Hey," Griffin said softly, standing behind the big kid.

Ben's brother turned and Griffin kicked him in the knee. I heard the bone crackle as the kid dropped to the ground with a scream. Griffin turned to Ben, who was now just getting to his feet. Griffin just stared at him, without saying a word.

Ben stood glowering a minute, then lowered his eyes. He reached down and helped his brother to his feet and the two of them limped and shuffled out of the alley.

Griffin looked at me and shook his head. "You're dumber than I thought."

"Dumber than *I* thought." I nodded.

He laughed, held out his hand to help me up. Blood spackled his palm.

I reached up. My hand had a cut from the garbage can lid. We clasped hands and he pulled me up to my feet. When he released my hand we were both smeared with blood.

He smiled. "Now we really are blood brothers, right, bro?"

29 ⌇

I *came out of the drugstore,* addressing the envelope as I walked.

"What are you doing?" he asked.

I ironed a wrinkled dollar bill against my thigh, slipped it into the envelope. I licked it closed. I dropped it in the mailbox outside Goodhart's Drugstore. It was addressed to Dr. Tom Askers.

"What the hell are you doing?" Griffin asked again.

"Paying a debt."

"That was our last dollar."

"Yeah."

"You're crazy, man," he said, but he didn't sound mad.

I guess he was right though. It didn't make sense to mail our last dollar off. But I needed to. It's hard to explain why, except that it was the first time since my trip to Hawaii that I recognized that I had a debt to Tom Askers. All this time I'd been figuring he owed *me* something. It wasn't until I slipped the envelope into the blue mailbox that I felt free of whoever I'd been before I came down here for the weekend. I wasn't thinking about Didra or Dad or Mom or anybody I'd known before this trip. I wasn't thinking about what they would do in this situation or what I was expected to do. Whatever would happen to Griffin and me after this morning, I wasn't going to blame anyone else.

Of course, I wasn't dumb enough to get rid of my ATM card.

We strolled slowly down the sleepy street.

"Where we going?" Griffin asked.

I didn't answer. It was the first time I wasn't asking him that question. The first time I wasn't looking for any answer.

We just kept walking. The sun was bright, brighter than you can imagine. It bounced off the glass windows of the stores and cars like a laser beam gone crazy. Every piece of glass or chrome or metal glittered like a flaming star. People were suddenly filling the streets, starting their day. We could be recognized at any minute. But somehow I knew we wouldn't be. It was like we were invisible. Like we were walking through this glittering galaxy of light all around us. Like we were living inside a star.

A jogger ran by us, checking the pulse at his throat. An old woman came out of her house, picked up the newspaper, read the front page headlines, shook her head, and went back inside. Two little black girls dressed in Sunday clothes were jumping rope until their mother came out and yelled at them for getting sweaty before church. A tailless cat rubbed against my leg, then jumped through an open window of a nearby house. A little girl inside the house scolded sternly, "Domino, where have you been?"

A white state police car was drifting down the street in

our direction. The sun slanted off the windshield, so we couldn't see the driver, couldn't tell if he was coming for us.

Griffin and I just kept walking. Walking and watching the people. As if we were seeing people for the first time. We weren't paddling to beat the current now, just floating along, floating with everyone else.

I was smiling now. I couldn't stop smiling. I looked over and Griffin was smiling too. I don't think either of us could have explained why we were smiling. We were fugitives on the run, wanted outlaws, I guess you could say. We had no money, no escape plan, no way out of our problems. The white police car was coming closer and closer. And yet here we were strolling down the Main Street sidewalk grinning like idiots, saying "Good morning" to everyone we passed. There was no reason, no logic, no rational explanation why. But there it was. Despite everything, we were happy. Go figure.

Raymond Obstfeld teaches literature and creative writing classes at Orange Coast College in Costa Mesa, California. He has written over thirty novels for adults, including *Dead Heat,* for which he was nominated for an Edgar Award by the Mystery Writers of America. He is also the author of a book of poetry, *The Cat with Half a Face;* two plays that have been produced; and several screenplays. His most recent book is entitled *Doing Good: A Guide to the Ethical and Moral Universe.* He lives in Irvine, California.